I0597959

Books in the Belinda Lawrence mystery series.

CAPABLE OF MURDER
THE EMBROIDERED CORPSE
BLOODY HAM
A CANTERBURY CRIME
A WICKED DESIGN
MURDER ON THE ISLAND

Author's website: http://beekayvic.tripod.com

FaceBook: www.facebook.com/brian.kavanagh.71

BRIAN KAVANAGH

MURDER

A BELINDA LAWRENCE MYSTERY

ON THE ISLAND

VIVID
PUBLISHING

Copyright © 2016 Brian Kavanagh

ISBN: 978-1-925442-03-8
Published by Vivid Publishing
P.O. Box 948, Fremantle
Western Australia 6959
www.vividpublishing.com.au

Cataloguing-in-Publication data is available from the National Library of Australia

For Adele

from: Belinda Lawrence
<bellaw@aqz1mail.com>
to: Mark Sallinger <marksalco@cxor822.com>
date: Wed, Feb 14, at 10:37 AM
subject: Please contact me.

Mark,
I would say, 'Dear Mark' but since your recent attitude and behaviour, I think not.
In your absence, I have been left to deal with your mother over the matter of our wedding plans, and you know how difficult that is. I am deeply hurt by you deserting me at this crucial time and as I have not had any communication from you since you left Guernsey for New York, I can only assume that your remarks to me reveal your true feelings.
On top of all that there has been a discovery that has the house in turmoil.

Your (ex?) fiancée,
Belinda.

Chapter One

"...and he snatched the newborn baby out of the arms of the midwife and threw it into the roaring fire!"

Belinda Lawrence gasped in horror and stood stock still. A footsore group of American tourists walking behind, unprepared for this sudden impediment to their excursion, bumped into her and muttering dark anti-Parisian crudities, discontentedly continued their way across the Pont Marie. Mark Sallinger turned back to his astonished fiancé. He smiled. "Did I shock you?"

Belinda moved to him and linked her arm through his. "Mark, that's a dreadful thing to say. Tossing a baby into a fire! You have a wicked mind."

They continued their way over the bridge towards the Ile St Louis. "But it's true, or at least the legend claims it is," said Mark, as they turned into the Rue St Louis en L'ile and meandered past the small shops, patisseries and boutique hotels.

"Well don't keep me in suspense, what's the full story?" said Belinda, "although I'm not so sure I want to hear it."

"Rubbish," said Mark, as he smiled at her, "you can't wait for the gory details."

"Get on with it."

"Well as I said, it was a dark and stormy night and –"

"– and the rain fell in torrents. Yes, I know, so –"

"But it *was* a dark and stormy night," said Mark defensively, "and if you don't be quiet, I won't tell you. As I said, it was in London, and there was a storm, and the year was somewhere about 1554, or thereabouts when an old midwife was woken up by someone knocking on the door. A man elbowed his way in and ordered the woman to come with him. He rushed her to a coach, and they drove off into the night. Soon London was far behind them, and although the woman could not see much, because of the dark, she knew they were in the country."

"Well if they were outside London, it would be a fair bet they'd be in the country," said Belinda teasingly.

Mark purposely ignored her interruption. "Finally the coach drove through the gateway to a large country house and the old woman was ushered into a gloomy bedroom, the only light came from some flickering candles and a blazing fire in the fireplace. On the bed, a young woman was in labour. The midwife was told to save the woman even if it meant the child died. The baby was born, and mother and child were doing well. But as the midwife was about to hand over the baby to its mother, the child was pulled from her arms. Then, as she watched in horror, the man hurled it into the roaring fire. In shock, the old woman was led away, a bag of coins given to her and a glass of wine."

Belinda gave a shiver. "I should think she'd need a drink after that experience."

"She was driven back to London and within a few days she was dead."

"Poisoned? The wine?" said Belinda.

Mark shrugged. "Possibly. But the interesting thing about this story is that before she died, she revealed the name of the woman who had given birth. Elizabeth."

Belinda looked at him. "Elizabeth I?"

"Well it certainly wasn't Elizabeth II," replied Mark mockingly. Belinda smiled and gave him a dig in the ribs with her elbow. A folk-tale, she thought to herself, but the image of the baby and the fire disturbed her. So absorbed with this fiction (for she wanted it to be fiction; to think otherwise would be too ghastly) she failed to notice the woman who exited from a nearby pharmacy and brushed past her. The woman joined a man who was waiting at a café. He rose to meet her and they hurried off onto the Pont Saint-Louis.

Belinda and Mark reached the end of the street and turned onto the Quai d' Orléans where their apartment was. The tiny rickety elevator carried them up and deposited them at the door of Mark's sister's apartment: Patricia and her husband had moved to New York for a month and Belinda and Mark had the use of it for a romantic Parisian holiday. Mark headed straight to the study and the computer; even a holiday, no matter how romantic, could stop the economic wheels of his business affairs. In the kitchen, Belinda poured a glass of orange juice.

"An email from mother," called Mark, "says she expects us tomorrow and not to be late."

Belinda walked to the study. "I wouldn't dare be. Not with your mother."

Mark smiled as he switched off the computer. "Oh come on, she's not that bad. A bit overpowering, I admit, but underneath –"

"Underneath she's a dictator," said Belinda with a smile. Belinda's relationship with her soon-to-be mother-in-law was an uneasy one, mainly because she knew that Melba, Lady Sallinger, as she now labelled herself, was of the old school and deemed her son should have married 'in his class' and not cohabit with a colonial. Not that she put it in those terms to Belinda's face, but it was often the subtext in their conversations.

Mark reached for his phone. "I'll get the car to collect us in the morning at, what? Say 8.00 am?"

"The ferry leaves St Malo at noon. Better make it 7.00," said Belinda, "we don't want to miss it and have to face your mother's wrath." She smiled and as Mark phoned to book the car she walked to the window. Below her flowed the Seine and, seemingly floating in the river, the Île de la Cité and the east end of Notre Dame with its fine display of flying buttresses. Beyond, the Latin Quarter and on the horizon the Panthéon, housing the remains of distinguished French citizens from Voltaire to Victor Hugo. Belinda smiled as she recalled, as a young tourist, her first visit to Paris and now, she was engaged, her future husband had a title and consequently she was to be, Lady Sallinger.

Not for the first time she considered the path her life had taken in the intervening ten years, from Australian teenage backpacker; to property owner when her murdered Great Aunt left her a cottage in Somerset; her friendship with the older Hazel Whitby and through her, an introduction into the world of buying and selling antiques.

She wondered how the next few days would be. The invitation from Melba to join her at her house on the island of Guernsey had come, more or less as a command, to plan their wedding. The fact her parents and Hazel Whitby were to be fellow guests provided some comfort for Belinda.

"Car booked. Hadn't we better pack?" Mark's question interrupted her thoughts, and she turned to the bedroom and began to sort out clothing.

"Just what is this house your mother has?"

"On Guernsey? An old Tudor house father bought some years ago. One of his companies initially bought it as an investment; had some idea of turning it into a boutique hotel, but time went on and they never got around to doing anything with it, so the old boy took it off their hands at a knock-down price, crafty old bugger. When he died, mother inherited it, and she has some crazy scheme about restoring it and retiring there.

"By the way, her email says we are to expect two additional guests. Some priest my mother argues theology with. Mother has a fixation with Rome and has been known to reduce the Holy See to tears. It's rumoured the Pope has been heard to plead, 'will no one rid me of this troublesome battle-axe?' And a writer, talking of troublesome; a woman doing research on the Nazi occupation of the island. Can't see those two providing much entertainment."

Belinda gave a murmur of acknowledgement and busied herself with packing. Her thoughts were scattered; the prospect of time spent with his mother, would they get on?

A Tudor house to explore; the freshness of the island of Guernsey off the coast of France.

An unexpected image flashed into her mind. Mark's tale of the midwife dragged from her bed in the middle of the night.

The baby thrown into the fire.

Belinda shivered. But the image stayed with her – like a horror movie. Repeating… repeating…

Chapter Two

Dowager Lady Sallinger, or as she preferred to be addressed, Melba, Lady Sallinger, removed her glasses and looked at Meg Giles - a look that instigated a tremor in the cook's stomach - a small, mouse-like woman with greying hair and a face set in permanent lines of disillusionment. Not for the first time did Melba wonder if she'd erred in employing this husband and wife team. He the gardener and the wife as the cook.

"There will be an additional guest staying this week, Mrs Giles." The tremor became a quake as Meg recalled the number of guests she was already expected to feed. Seven. Plus the residents of the house.

Lady Sallinger glanced at the letter in her hand. "A Mr Harvey, a designer, will be arriving this evening, so that will be nine for dinner."

"Yes, M'Lady," replied Meg, quickly reviewing her planned menu. Soup, Steak pie, potatoes, greens, and steamed pudding. Should be able to stretch it to another mouth.

"One thing," continued Lady Sallinger, "Mr Harvey is a vegetarian and prefers salads. I imagine that will not present a problem?"

Meg's heart sank.

"And I also see from his dietary requirements, he does not eat anything with sugar," continued Lady Sallinger, peering at the letter through her glasses. "Really, the things one is expected to provide for guests. In my day, they took what they were given and put up with it. But this gentleman comes highly recommended, and I need his services in restoring the house, so salads it must be." She noticed the worried expression on the cook's face. "Mrs Giles, I hope you aren't going to tell me there will be a difficulty." This was not a question, more like a requirement.

"I think I can manage a small salad this evening, M'Lady, lettuce, tomatoes and things, but there were no cucumbers at the market this morning, I looked twice."

Lady Sallinger had already lost interest and reached for a magazine devoted to restoring bathrooms. "That should suffice. No doubt you will be able to obtain further vegetarian accessories tomorrow. That will be all."

Meg gave a bob before the elderly, tall domineering woman seated before her. The sun shone on silver hair where a single strand out of place was never to be tolerated, dark piercing eyes, sheltered now behind cat eye styled glasses that garnished a permanent haughty expression designed to intimidate anyone foolish enough to offer a challenge. Wondering if she and her husband had made a mistake in taking on this job, Meg retired to the kitchen, where she promptly downed a glass of cooking sherry and set about planning delicious ways in which she could maim Lady Sallinger for life.

In another part of the house, in her room, Ms Angela Massey gazed at her reflection in a mirror. Today was the 13th. Her birthday. 70 years. Her face revealed those years with heavy lines gouged deep and numerous. Guilt? Sorrow? Maybe both. She inspected her reflection more closely. Hooded eyes had faded to a dull grey, her hair still held much of its original darkness. Her mouth now thin and vinegary. She glanced down at her body, heavier now than in those days. Was it so many years ago that it happened? With a grunt of dismissal, she threw the mirror onto the bed and lifted a typewritten list. The guest list, she as the housekeeper, had received from Lady Sallinger. In all the years she'd served in this position, she'd been required to maintain the property, with only the occasional visitor. Much had changed since it ceased to be a company investment property when sold to Sir Randolph. With him now dead his widow was making noises about retiring to the house, and also, modernising it. Ms Massey liked the old Tudor house for what it was and as it was. Thoughts of giving notice flittered through her mind again but quickly faded as she remembered the special bond she had with the old building.

The waters of the English Channel were calm on the journey from France to the island of Guernsey and Belinda had enjoyed the novelty of sea travel, wrapped as she had been in Mark's strong embrace. Another traveller watching them would have seen a couple outwardly in love; he, a strong masculine figure, with the demeanour of a man who knows what he wants and is certain he will get it. Well groomed, handsome with grey just dusting his full head of dark hair: her, a woman in her prime, elegant, with an engaging smile that suggested a sense of humour and a willingness to engage in adventure. Her chestnut hair shaped in the latest fashion stirred in the sea breeze, and her blue eyes were alert with curiosity. The diamond ring on her finger verified her as a prospective bride. Yet there was an air of unease about her as the sleek ferry glided into St Peter Port.

Trivial steely grey clouds on the horizon suggested a change in the weather, but for now, sunshine bathed the Port and the nearby island of Sark. Stepping onto the wharf the white facades of nearby buildings dazzled Belinda. A stocky, red-faced man shuffled towards Mark. Tanned arms suggested a life in the open. Dressed in worn jeans, shirt and a rather threadbare waistcoat, he gave a nervous smile. "Would I be addressing Sir Mark?"

Mark glanced over the rim of his sunglasses. "Yes, that's right. You are...?"

"Name's Joe Giles, Sir. Lady Sallinger's gardener. M'Lady sent me to collect you and drive you to the Lodge." He smiled at Belinda. "Might I offer my congratulations, M'Lady of your forthcoming nuptials."

Belinda smiled back. "Thank you Mr Giles, but I have no title as yet. Just Ms Lawrence for the moment."

Joe tapped his forehead. "Beg pardon, Miss. Seems I jumped the gun, so to speak. Now if you'll follow me, I'll take you to the car." So saying he bent down, picked up their suitcases and shuffled off, his uneven gait impeded by the luggage. Belinda and Mark exchanged a smile and followed in his footsteps.

He led them to a gleaming black& white, four-door Bentley Consort. Mark gave a delighted chuckle. "I haven't seen this old girl since I was a boy. It's been up on blocks as long as I can remember."

"Her Ladyship had it restored and shipped to the island. 'Says it was her husband's favourite car. Bought it just after they married, she says." Joe placed their luggage in the boot. They took their places in the car, and Belinda smiled at the leather and polished wood interior.

"That's right," said Mark, "my sister and I always looked forward to picnics, with my father at the wheel and my mother a skilled 'back seat driver'."

The elegant saloon, with Joe at the wheel, soon left the Port behind and glided smoothly inland where green fields, lined with voluptuous trees, stretched before them vibrant in the afternoon sun. Joe slowed the car and turned into an isolated side lane. Through the trees, Belinda caught her first glimpse of the house. Large and shimmering, the black and white timber/ plaster construction was a picture postcard image of a Tudor farmhouse.

As they approached, Belinda had an uneasy feeling; an unidentified sense of despair, fear of an intangible menace. On the surface, the old house appeared to be idyllic with its tiled roof, herringbone timber-frame, leaded mullioned windows and gabled eaves. The west end of the building sagged a little from age, but generally the two-story structure stood proud, with four attic windows, its eyes watching over all. There was evidence of a neglected garden, which showed signs of recent repair. So what could be threatening about it, Belinda asked herself. But as the car drew to a halt at the front door, it seemed the building had grown into a grotesque parody of a Tudor mansion. She had to steel herself to clamber from the car and face the building. But as she did the feeling of doom melted away and she saw the house for what it was.

The massive, nail-studded plank door swung open, and a familiar voice filled the air. "Thank God you're here. I feel as though I'm at a geriatrics convention."

Hazel Whitby, dressed in a stylish ensemble consisting of a scarlet poncho, black leggings and a black knitted sweater, hugged Belinda to her. "I mean, I really love your darling parents, Bel, but your father seems to nod off at the most inconvenient times, and your mum is too inquisitive and cheerful to be real." She glanced at Mark. "And as for the Dowager Lady, I suspect in a past life your mother was Madame Defarge. Give her a couple of knitting needles and watch the heads roll."

Belinda laughed, happy to see her old friend. "When did you arrive?"

"Flew in yesterday afternoon," said Hazel, indicating that Mark should take their suitcases inside. Hazel, a woman of 'a certain age', had been Belinda's friend now for many years, and with her tall, well-preserved figure and natural insouciance, added fun and amusement to Belinda's life. She tossed back her long black hair, took Belinda by the arm and together the two friends entered the house. "Getting your old dad on the plane was a trial. 'Didn't seem to know what was going on." She leaned closer to Belinda and whispered in her ear, "I've got something to tell you. There's something going on in this house. Something very odd." They arrived in a spacious wood-panelled entrance hall with a large stone fireplace and a dog-leg staircase leading to the floor above. There was a perfume comprised of old roses, apples and the scent of past centuries. Off to the right Belinda caught a glimpse of a well-furnished, dark reception room and heard the voice of her future mother-in-law.

From on the staircase, a tall woman dressed in black descended and made her way to them. "Good afternoon, Miss. Welcome to The Lodge. I'm Ms Massey, her Ladyship's housekeeper." Belinda acknowledged the woman's welcome but felt there was little warmth in the greeting. Belinda guessed Ms Massey to be in her seventies, straggly hair and a bitter expression, which hinted at a dark personality her sombre dress did nothing to dispel.

"Sir Mark," continued Ms Massey, "I will have your bags sent to your room upstairs. The west wing of the house is closed off; parts of it are unsafe because of structural faults, due to the age of the building. Her ladyship is intent on restoring it, but I'm sure you'll be comfortable in the room I have prepared for you. " She turned and walked to the larger room. "Her Ladyship asked that you attend her in the Drawing Room upon your arrival." The trio followed and Ms Massey, having performed her welcoming duty retreated, but after a few steps, turned and watched the new arrivals as they entered the large reception room and approached Lady Sallinger. To her mind, the new arrivals were not welcome, and the other guests due to arrive later in the day more of a threat. Ms Massey did not like the way things were happening at the Lodge; her mind raced as she considered the unwanted intrusion.

Chapter Three

Father Ignatius put aside his breviary and watched St Peter Port drift closer as the ferry from Portsmouth completed the ocean crossing. The late after-noon light had thrown a soft gilt sheen onto the white buildings lining the docks. Few passengers had embarked on the remarkably calm passage; now they left their seats and crowded near the doors eager to disembark. Father Ignatius brushed some crumbs, remnants of a biscuit consumed with his coffee so that his black suit regained its usual immaculate charisma. He ran a finger inside his white Roman Collar and stretched his neck. To an observer it was almost as though he was new to it, but the flecks of grey in his hair and the calm he exuded gave a lie to that assumption and he presented as a man in his forties who had given his life to the service of God.

Across the aisle from him a slim, well-preserved woman who could have been aged fifty was attending to her makeup. He had glanced at her earlier in the voyage. She was startlingly beautiful with carefully coiffured blond hair and an elegance that suggested good breeding and good taste. She snapped her compact shut with a click, dropped it in her bag and rose to make her way to the door. As she did, she glanced in his direction. The priest gave a slight smile. The woman dropped her eyes, but the shadow of a grin flashed across her features. Father Ignatius dumped the breviary in his carry case and rose to follow the woman.

Stepping out on the quay he took in his surroundings. Beyond the ferry, he could see Castle Cornet, Guernsey's ancient royal fortress, standing guard for close on eight centuries. He glanced at his watch and wondered if Lady Sallinger had remembered to send her car to collect him. No sooner had he the thought, when a rustic figure approached, hat in hand.

"You'd be the Reverend gentleman, is my guess. I'm Joe Giles, and I'm to drive you to the Lodge." He collected the priest's luggage and shambled off towards an impressive vintage Bentley. Father Ignatius followed and, as Joe placed the bags in the boot, opened the car door. To his surprise, the woman who had been on the ferry was seated in the back. She gave him an unwelcoming glance. The priest clambered in and took his place beside her.

"This is a pleasant surprise. I take it you are to be a guest of Melba's?"

The woman gave a faint nod. "Of Lady Sallinger, yes." She remained aloof and as the car began its journey, transferred her gaze to the activity on the wharf.

Undaunted Father Ignatius continued. "Melba, or Lady Sallinger if you prefer, has for some time shown great interest in the Church of Rome, and I have been advising her."

The woman turned back to him and held his gaze. "Are you a Jesuit?" The priest looked askance. "In that case, I suggest you are a trouble maker," the woman continued, "you have a history of seeking power and political intrigues."

Father Ignatius gave a self-deprecating smile and nodded. "That is how the world prefers to view us, I admit. But what brings you to Guernsey and, in particular, to Melba, Lady Sallinger's house?"

The woman twisted a ruby ring on her finger. "I'm writing a book about the history of Guernsey and the German occupation of the Island during World War II. Lady Sallinger was kind enough to invite me to stay with her while I do my research."

"If we are to be companions, as it were, at least during our stay, I should introduce myself,

Father Ignatius of the Society of Jesus. And you?"

The woman hesitated a moment. "Catherine Foster."

The priest reached into his carry case and unwrapped a large candle. "This is a gift for our hostess. A Paschal Candle sometimes referred to as the Easter candle." He held it up for Catherine to admire. It was about two feet long and four inches in diameter, with an ornate cross adorning the creamy wax surface. "Do you think she'll like it?"

Catherine gave a passing glance at the candle. "I'm sure someone will find a use for it." With that, she brought the conversation to an end and turned to look at the passing scenery. Father Ignatius sank back in his seat and did likewise.

Joe Giles, having heard this exchange, glanced in the rear vision mirror at his passengers. "S'truth, her Ladyship picks some weird birds," he said to himself, "the Lodge'll be like a looney bin this week."

Chapter Four

"Mark, you will be pleased to know that I have arranged for your marriage to be celebrated in St Margaret's Westminster on the 23rd of next month."

Belinda's teacup clattered onto the saucer. "St Margaret's?"

Lady Sallinger paused in her duties as hostess while pouring a cup of tea and scrutinised Belinda as though she had committed some adolescent social indiscretion. Resuming pouring, she continued in a voice, the construction of which had many of the elements of steel. "The very same. *I* was married there. My *parents* were married there. My *daughter* was married there. It is only fitting that my *son* should also be."

There was a strained silence as Lady Sallinger handed the tea to Ms Massey, who in turn, gave it to Belinda's mother, a small bird-like woman wearing a bright yellow beret.

The group seated in the Drawing Room, around the afternoon-tea re-past exchanged furtive glances, all except Belinda's father, a large elderly man with a cheery expression, who was engaged in eating a scone, which he had engulfed in strawberry jam and clotted cream.

Hazel bit her lip to hide a smile and took an unexpected interest in the heavily beamed ceiling.

Mrs Lawrence looked bewildered and scrutinised the Aubusson carpet.

Catherine Foster raised an eyebrow before transferring her gaze to the linen-fold wood panelling surrounding the fireplace.

Mark frowned and looked with concern to Belinda, who stared at his mother in total disbelief.

Ms Massey glided from the room to linger like a shadow in the entrance hall.

Father Ignatius cleared his throat. "Yes, St Margaret's, Westminster, dedicated to Margaret of Antioch. Curiously she is celebrated as a saint by the Roman Catholic, Anglican Churches, and the Orthodox Church. However, there is little to prove her existence, and –"

"Thank you, Father," interrupted Melba, "I'm sure we are all pleased that so many religions have mingled in this instance and not resorted to calumny. Now," she turned to Mark, "the reception will be held in the cloisters of the Abbey. I believe they do a tolerable table there."

Belinda glanced at Mark, who sighed, placed his teacup on a nearby table and addressed his mother.

"I don't believe her!" Belinda shouted through tense lips. She, her mother, and Hazel had escaped the alarums and excursions now developing between mother and son, the vibration of which broke through the Tudor diamond glass windows. The three women moved away from the house and into the relative quiet of the garden. Mr Lawrence, at his wife's insistence, had retired to his room for a nap; Father Ignatius and Catherine Foster had hurriedly left the scene of the family squabble and gone their separate ways in the house.

"Does she really think she can take over my marriage and expect me just to go along with what she wants?" Belinda continued, her anger growing stronger by the minute. Her companions remained silent. Her mother shaking her head with worry. Hazel watching Joe Giles as he dug out shrubs growing near the house.

Belinda eventually sank into a brooding silence. Hazel glanced at her, and in an attempt to distract her from the ongoing combat indoors put an arm around her shoulder. "Remember I said something odd was happening here?" Belinda was silent, still raging at the treatment from Mark's mother. Hazel gave her a hug. "Have you noticed anything strange about the housekeeper?"

"Ms Massey?" replied Mrs Lawrence. "I have. 'Found her in our bedroom last night when we went up after supper. 'Said she'd had been placing some fresh towels, but that was a lie. The towels were there when we arrived. I think she'd been going through our things."

"I caught her in my room as well," said Hazel, "she claimed she was just making sure I had everything I needed, and hurried away before I could question her further. I suspected she was planning to search my luggage, but I interrupted her before she had a chance."

The conversation began to sink into Belinda's mind, and she turned back to Hazel.

"What was that you said?"

"But even odder, continued Hazel, "I woke in the middle of the night, about two, I guess, and I could hear someone crying."

"Crying?" said Belinda.

"Well more like sobbing. I got up and went out into the passage. It was pitch black, and I had to feel my way along to the landing. The sobbing seemed to come from up in the attic rooms, where it appears Ms Massey sleeps. I was about to try and climb the stairs to see if she was all right, when there was a noise on the main staircase, as though someone was climbing. I felt my way back to my room and waited in the dark, but from then on it was silent."

"Well it wasn't Mr Lawrence or me, roaming around in the dark," said Belinda's mother, "he sleeps like a log. Maybe the cook or the gardener?"

"No, they live in the cottage in the grounds, and why would they be wandering around in the middle of the night?"

"Now that I think about it," said Mrs Lawrence, "I did hear the sobbing, very faintly. I wondered if it was Melba, but her rooms are at the other end of the house, and she doesn't strike me as a woman who's given to crying. More likely she causes it."

"And another peculiar thing," said Hazel, "twice now I've caught Ms Massey standing at the window staring at the gardener as he digs up the garden. When she saw me watching her, she turned on her heel and walked off without a word."

Belinda gave a little shrug. "Maybe she's just watching to make sure he does his job. But about the –"

Before she could continue, Mark burst out of the house and thundered towards them, his hands formed into tight fists and his face red with anger. "My mother is being her bloody-minded best! She won't listen to reason and insists we do what she wants, damn her. Damn her to hell!"

"My sentiments as well," said Hazel.

"What can we do," asked Belinda, "we wanted just a quiet, small wedding, and now..."

Mark gave a sigh. "Now we'll just have to spend time trying to convince her to see it our way."

The sound of a car driving into the garden distracted them, and they turned to watch as a bright red sports car came to a halt. The engine purred to silence and a young man, handsome, tanned and the image of dangerous masculinity, emerged from the car.

Belinda felt Hazel's arms fall from her shoulder and sensed her friend slipping into her beddable disposition.

The man smiled at the group, dazzling white teeth glowing in the late afternoon sun.

Marchmain Harvey had arrived.

Chapter Five

"And then, of course, there are The Guernsey Martyrs," said Father Ignatius, "that was rather an unfortunate episode."

The evening meal had been a tense affair with hardly a word spoken between Melba, Belinda, and Mark. The remaining guests carried on a fractured conversation, detailing the weather, the history of the house, tentative plans to explore the island, while Hazel devoted herself entirely to Marchmain Harvey and had been enthusiastically encouraged to call him, 'Manny'. "That's what I'm known as 'round Knightsbridge," he grinned, as he demolished his makeshift salad. Hazel was prepared to call him anything he wanted including gorgeous, or preferably, 'mine'.

A depleted group now sat in the Drawing Room, the dim lighting creating a faintly sinister atmosphere. To Hazel's chagrin, Melba had carried Manny off to another part of the building to begin plans for the restoration of the Lodge. Belinda's parents had retired for the night, and Mark was in his room engrossed in international business details on his computer; so a small group of four remained, a carafe of

Port sustaining them as the clock struck midnight.

"The Guernsey martyrs? What are they?" asked Belinda.

"Three women who were executed in 1556."

"Executed?" said Hazel, topping up her glass. It was splendid Port. "Why was that?"

"A complicated case," said Father Ignatius, "with an intriguing background. It took place during the tumultuous times of the Reformation, or more accurately as a result of the Reformation."

"After Henry VIII broke with Rome and declared himself head of the Church in England?"

"That's right. His son Edward continued in that role, but the changeover from the old faith was not a smooth transition. Many of the people, particularly those in country areas didn't take kindly to having Protestantism thrust on them. They were quite happy as they were with their regional feast days. The village priest was more or less on their pay role to perform his duties and the local church was the villager's domain; the various guilds provided for upkeep, installed religious items, and local women made vestments and altar coverings, all as part of their faith."

"But they were expected to conform to the new religion, weren't they?" said Catherine Foster. Belinda glanced at her. She had been reading a history of the Nazi invasion and had hardly spoken a word all evening. Now she was frowning and massaging her cheek.

"Yes," said Father Ignatius, "that was the general idea, but it was difficult to implement, except by force, and things got muddier when Edward died and his sister, Mary came to the throne."

"She was still Catholic," said Hazel.

"And that put the cat among the pigeons," replied the priest. "Mary returned the country to the Old Faith, the Church of Rome."

"Does this have anything to do with the execution of the three women?" said Belinda.

"Everything."

The chink of silver teaspoons on bone china and the rich aroma of coffee proclaimed the arrival of Ms Massey.

"I thought as you are sitting up late, you'd like some fresh coffee."

Father Ignatius watched her carefully as she poured the coffee. When she handed a cup to him, he said, "Massey. That's an interesting name, don't you agree?"

Ms Massey hesitated, looked him in the eye before turning back to resume pouring coffee. "A name that has connections to Guernsey, Ms Massey, which I'm sure you're aware of. Do you come from this part of the world?"

Ms Massey turned from handing a cup to Belinda. "No, Father. I come from London. Now if you'll excuse me." She turned and hurried from the room. Belinda and Hazel exchanged a look. Catherine closed her book reached for her coffee, sat back in her chair and murmured, "I thought as much."

"So, Father, what's the connection with the name, Massey?" said Belinda.

"It goes back to the Guernsey Martyrs I mentioned. During the sixteenth century, Guernsey was divided. Some observed the old Roman Catholic faith and others Protestantism. Queen Mary I was on the throne at the time and was a Catholic. It was then that the executions took place. A woman called Vincente Gosset was brought before the Bailiff."

"On what charge," asked Hazel.

"Of having stolen a silver cup from a house here in Peter-Port. Now this is where the name, Massey comes into the story. Having taken the cup, the woman took it to another woman a neighbour named, Perotine Massey. She wanted money for it, sixpence I think was the price asked."

"Cheap at half the price," said Hazel, with a grin.

"But Massey suspected the cup was hot and, what's more, she believed she knew who it belonged to. So instead of forking out sixpence she reported the theft."

"Charming. Dropping her neighbour right in it," said Hazel.

"But there was some poetic justice. After Gosset confessed to the pocketing of the cup, the Constable of the town, called at Massey's house in regard to the case, where he spied a number of pewter bowls which he questioned the ownership of and so had all the residents of the Massey house bundled off to Castle Cornet and held in prison there. The prisoners consisted of Massey, her mother Catherine Cauché, and her sister Guillemine Guilbert."

Belinda thought the priest was long winded in telling his tale. "So when do the martyrs come into the story?" She tried to stifle a yawn.

The priest turned to her. "It was after the trial and the three women were convicted and condemned to be burned at the stake, when..."

Heavy footsteps on the staircase brought Mark unexpectedly into the room. All eyes turned on him. He moved swiftly to Belinda and put his hands on her shoulders.

"Sweetheart, bad news. I'm afraid I have to leave."

Mark clicked his suitcase shut. It was 1.00am and Belinda, confused and angry, stared at him across the bed.

"I've told you a dozen times, Bel. I have to be in New York as soon as possible. I've arranged for a company jet to collect me here at 6.00AM to get back to London and then onto the States so I would like to get a few hours sleep. Now if you'll just stop questioning me –

"No I won't stop," said Belinda, harshly. "Why should I? We are supposed to be arranging a rather important event in our lives – marriage – and you just decide to up and off leaving me to deal with it all and what's more, negotiate with your mother when you know she doesn't like me."

Mark gave a sigh of irritation. "Bel, we are in serious trouble and unless the problem is resolved, there may not be a wedding."

Belinda felt the words as a physical blow. "What?"

"I mean you may not want to marry me. I've been notified of deception in one of my companies in the States. Auditors have discovered an estimated one billion dollars' worth of fraud. If I don't deal with it now, it could affect my other companies, and not only me but all the employees. Unless I manage it now there's a strong possibility that I may not have any money, and you wouldn't want to marry a pauper, would you?"

Belinda looked at him as though seeing him for the first time. "Is that why you thought I'd marry you? For your money?"

Mark didn't reply, but closed his laptop and placed it in his briefcase. His silence was the answer to her question.

Chapter Six

The sound of the front door closing brought Belinda from a troubled slumber to hear a car door close and an engine spring into life. Belinda looked around her. The Drawing Room where she'd spent the last few hours was saturated with pale early morning light. She uncurled herself from the foetal position she had finally dozed off in and rose from the sofa. Through the window, she saw the taxi Mark had called, as it left the garden and turned onto the main road.

The sudden awareness of a presence nearby made her turn. In the shadowy doorway stood Ms Massey, wraith-like in her dark dress and sallow complexion.

"Good morning, Miss. Is there anything you need?"

Belinda shook her head, but as the woman turned away, she said, "Coffee. I'd like some coffee if it's not too much trouble."

Ms Massey inclined her head in deference and retreated into the passageway.

Belinda stretched her arms above her head. The sofa, while comfortable, hadn't been the ideal bed and what little sleep she'd had had left her crumpled and weary. Ms Massey returned with a tray bearing a jug of coffee and a cup. Belinda thanked her and poured the coffee. The restorative liquid began to ease her tension. Ms Massey stood by, inquisitive eyes fixed firmly on Belinda.

"I found you sleeping on the sofa, Miss, when I rose early. Is there a problem with your bed?"

Belinda gave a cynical smirk. "You could say that."

"I can arrange for you to have another room, Miss, if there is a problem."

"The problem is not in the room, I'm afraid." Then half to herself she muttered, "He's not in the house." Aware then that it had nothing to do with Ms Massey, she said, "Sir Mark has had to go to New York on urgent business."

Ms Massey's expression was solemn. "I'll let M'Lady know."

"No,' said Belinda reluctantly, "I'll do that. I have to talk to her anyway."

Ms Massey gave a nod of acceptance and withdrew. On the way back to the kitchen, she thought over the recent development. She had heard the raised voices of Sir Mark and Belinda and had crept down from her attic room to listen at their bedroom door. As Belinda had stormed out she almost collided with Ms

Massey, but it was obvious she was so distressed she was unaware of her presence and Ms Massey was able to blend into the shadows and return to her room to mull over this development

Now in the kitchen, she brewed a pot of tea. Meg Giles would not arrive to begin preparing for breakfast until seven. In the early morning quiet, she sipped her tea and speculated on the likelihood of the guests departing, at least those associated with the wedding plans. Surely the couple would not kiss and make up? But that would leave the priest, the woman writing about the Germans and the interior decorator. With the exception of the latter, they were likely to move on soon and hopefully things would return to normal.

The sound of an approaching engine disturbed her thoughts and glancing out the window she saw Joe Giles seated in the cabin of a small Bobcat as he drove it into the rear garden, the rubber tracks digging deep into the already cleared beds. Before it, a large metal bucket with sharp, angry teeth swayed from the jointed arm; to Ms Massey it suggested an avenging angel. She gave a shiver of fear.

"You had better get used to it, my girl." Melba, Lady Sallinger spread thick-cut marmalade on her toast and proceeded to crunch it between somewhat stained dentures. Belinda sat facing her across the small table which crowded a Victorian loveseat, various chairs, an antique Singer sewing machine on which reposed a laptop, an anachronism in this ripened setting, a cabinet overcrowded with chipped porcelain, grim vases, heavily tarnished flatware, all of which might be described as jetsam, (jettisoned by someone in distress, thought Belinda).

Melba noticed her critical appraisal of the cabinet's faded contents. "Revolting rubbish. Decades of poor taste from provincial owners. I've told Mrs Giles to remove it all to a Charity Shop. Doubtless some poor individuals will find something they value." Another mouthful of toast disappeared.

From outside the roar of the motor was heard as Joe Giles began his excavation work in the garden. Melba seemed oblivious of this. Through the window, Belinda could see the machine going to and fro, the metal bucket carrying fresh dug soil to return empty, eager to plunge into the earth once again. The meeting with her future mother-in-law took place in

Melba's morning room, where the lady in question was consuming her breakfast with fervour. The other guests were ingesting their breakfast in the dining room where, Belinda assumed, the matter of Mark's sudden departure after their loud quarrel had replaced the banalities of the weather forecast.

Her dentures having completed their task, Melba took a sip of tea, dabbed her mouth with a lace napkin, and turned her attention to Belinda.

"If you are to marry my son you must expect that he will fly off without a moment's notice."

Belinda's mouth was open in reply to this foolishness when both women were distracted by the sounds of distress coming from the dining room. Rapid footsteps approached, the door opened and a nervous Meg Giles, tugging fretfully at her apron, gave a bob to Melba. "Beg pardon, M'Lady, Joe has found something. Something he wants you to see."

Before Melba could reply, Joe appeared behind his wife, cap in hand. Melba glanced in dismay at his muddied boots on the carpet. "Well? What is it?"

"I think you'd best come and look, M'Lady."

"Look at what?" asked Melba, crossly.

"What I found –"

"And what is that?" demanded Melba.

"A skeleton, M'Lady. The skeleton of a baby."

Chapter Seven

The tiny skeleton lay on its side, fragile fingers clasped in front of the skull in an attitude of prayer. Soil from the recent excavation buried the lower limbs. All members of the household stood surrounding the small grave and gazed at the long-dead infant. Belinda gave a sob and turned away. Ms Massey stood behind her and their eyes met. Something in Ms Massey's gaze alarmed her; was it shock? Compassion? Or...repugnance?

Lady Sallinger turned and stepped away from the grave. "Humph. Given the age of this building, no doubt the child was buried sometime long ago during its history. Probably a servant girl in trouble and buried the child here to save her job. Not an uncommon occurrence. Best just cover it up and get on with clearing the garden."

The others glanced at each other, resentful of Melba's lack of sympathy. Hazel stepped closer to the grave. "It looks as though it was newborn." Beneath the skeleton, a scrap of fabric poked through the soil. "There's some sort of material under the bones," she said. "It could prove to be a clue."

Melba turned back, annoyed by this intrusion into her ordered day. "Rubbish, in all likelihood just part of the serving girl's apron or skirt. I tell you it's probably Tudor. Hundreds of years old."

Marchmain stepped closer to the skeleton and took several photos with his phone. He glanced at the recorded images and slipped the phone into his pocket.

Melba led the charge back to the house, with the others following slowly, each absorbed in speculation about the origins of the skeleton.

Belinda caught up with Father Ignatius. "Father, surely we can't just bury the poor thing again?"

The priest gave a nod of agreement. "I do believe the police should be informed. However Melba thinks otherwise, so perhaps it is best not to upset her."

Belinda looked at him in disbelief and gave a snort of derision. "Really? Well, I'm just in the mood to upset her."

"How long ago did Mark's father buy the Lodge?" Hazel had hired a car and driven Belinda down to Saint Peter Port, partly to distract her from the quarrel with Mark and his departure, and partly to get her away from the house and out of Melba's reach. After admiring the Bailiwick of Guernsey Millennium Tapestry, an embroidered canvas work illustrating 1000 years of local history, they were coming to the end of the tour.

"I think only about five years ago," said Belinda distractedly, "but before that, one of his companies owned it. Before that, it was owned by some titled family with hazy royal connections and used as a holiday house."

"So the baby could have been born at any time to anyone?"

"Or just buried there. It could have been born anywhere."

The police had arrived and after questioning everyone at the Lodge, had taken the pitiful remains away for forensic examination. The general consensus was the burial had taken place some time ago and historical records relating to the various owners of the house would be examined.

Melba was speechless with horror, firstly that the police were actually a presence in her house, and secondly that someone had dared to disobey her instructions. Her discovery that that 'someone' was Belinda had brought on a severe attack of angina, forcing her to retire to her room but had left a command for Belinda to attend her at seven that evening.

Late in the afternoon Belinda and Hazel meandered along the streets, Belinda in a glum mood still dealing with Mark's desertion; Hazel's mood more prosaic, anticipating a gin and tonic. With luck, they soon stumbled on a small bar and took their place near the window. Suitably refreshed, Hazel began to check out the locals as they went about their business in the nearby street. Among the crowd, she was surprised to see Catherine Foster. She nudged Belinda and pointed. "There's our historian."

They watched as Catherine hurried by, glancing now and then at a scrap of paper in her hand. She seemed distracted but paused outside a small second-hand book shop, removed her sunglasses, checked the street number against the paper, decided this was the address she wanted and, avoiding a battered motorbike leaning against the window, opened the door and entered.

"Wonder what she wants in there? Research? "said Belinda.

"On the German wartime invasion? Maybe, but I would have thought she'd get all the research she wanted at the German occupation museum they have here. I hear it's excellent," replied Hazel, as the welcome gin began its spirited restoration.

"Did you see she has a limp? Only a very slight one. I hadn't noticed that before."

"Genetic do you think or an accident?"

Belinda shrugged. "Who can tell. Pity, as she's such an attractive woman. How old do you think she is?"

"Somewhere about fifty. But she's had a facelift."

"Oh? How can you tell?"

Hazel gave the remnants of her gin a stir with the swizzle stick. "Well for starters, she has no turkey neck. Once you hit fifty, which is one of the horrors awaiting you, little lady, the skin of the neck droops, and lo and behold, you have a gobbler." As she said it, she self-consciously massaged the flesh under her chin. The prognostication was not good. "Surgery gets rid of that," she added thoughtfully, wondering if she should make an appointment with a Harley Street clinic on her return to London. "And have you noticed her ears? You can't have a facelift without having a scar in front of each ear. And she has a patch of smooth, light coloured skin on her ears which is different from the fine wrinkly skin on her cheeks."

"How do you know these things," laughed Belinda.

"Conscientious study," said Hazel, in all sincerity. Preservation of her physical attributes was high on her agenda. "Also, our researcher has had a nose job. A silicone implant probably. Any foreign material added underneath the skin tends not to blend smoothly so at some angles it's visible, and you can see a slight depression between the silicone and the rest of her nose."

Belinda was amused at her friend's interest in cosmetic surgery, but to Hazel, it was seeking out her enemy's imperfections, as she considered the possibility Catherine could be a potential adversary in her pursuit for the affections of Marchmain Harvey.

Their gaze returned to the street and another familiar figure appeared. It was Father Ignatius. He had ditched his clerical dog collar and was dressed in black trousers and a black short-sleeved, open-necked shirt. He was strolling casually looking in shop windows, the perfect image of a tourist taking in the sights. His ambling eventually brought him to the second-hand bookshop. Here he halted, but not looking in the window he glanced up and down the street, turned on his heel and entered the shop.

"Well, coincidence? I think not," said Belinda.

"Do you think our priest is about to break his vow of chastity?" said Hazel, indicating to the barman they needed further refreshments. "They arrived together on the same ferry."

"That could have been a coincidence. But this looks like an assignation."

"A tryst?"

"Call it what you like but it does seem they arranged to meet in the book shop."

"Let's wait and see what happens when they come out," said Hazel, as the barman appeared at her elbow bearing the elixir of life. "You know, I've been thinking about that skeleton. I wish I'd taken a closer look."

Belinda glanced at her. "Why?"

"Not sure. But something's bugging me about it. And why was that old biddy, Melba so keen for us to forget about it and cover it up? Why the insistence that it was hundreds of years old?"

"Ms Massey seemed distraught."

"Hmm, probably just shock. Still, she's an odd bird."

"It's also strange that no-one challenged Melba but went along so willingly with what she wanted."

Hazel gave a grin. "That is until you stuck your oar in."

Belinda gave a shrug. What would happen when she had to confront Melba that evening and explain her action in notifying the police? It should prove to be volatile.

As if reading her thoughts, Hazel said, "I'd give anything to be a fly on the wall for that face-off with Melba."

Belinda laughed. "I fully expect you to have your ear glued firmly to the keyhole."

For the next ten minutes, they sipped their gins each speculating on the meaning of what had happened, alerted suddenly when the door of the bookshop opened and Father Ignatius appeared. He strode off in the direction of the harbour. A few minutes later Catherine stepped into the street, adjusted her sunglasses and meandered off in the opposite direction.

Belinda and Hazel exchanged a glance. They didn't need to think what their next move was to be. Hazel gulped the last of her gin and they left the bar and made for the book shop.

Chapter Eight

Above the shop door, Belinda saw a sign 'Proprietor M. Miller'. A bell attached to the door gave a tinkle when they entered, thereby announcing a potential customer. A shadowy figure seated behind a counter squinted up briefly from a computer and gave a judgelike frown.

"Excuse me," said Hazel, "we were to meet some friends of ours here, but I'm afraid we're running late."

The man was not distracted from his noisy computer game. "Oh, yes?"

"A couple," said Hazel undeterred, "a man and a woman, a blonde woman. Have they been here?"

Finally, the man glanced up from his game. "You've just missed them. They left a few minutes ago. 'Surprised you didn't pass each other on the street." His voice was husky and the pungent smell that dwells on heavy smokers, caused Hazel, an ex-smoker, to shrink a little with the realisation that until recently she'd exuded a similar malodorous stench, which all the perfumes in Arabia - not to mention the annual output of a Parisian parfumerie - could not sweeten.

"Oh, what a nuisance," she said, gagging a little, "he was to show us a book he was interested in. Do you know what that was?"

The man shifted in his seat and into the light. They could see he was about forty, solidly built, dark hair, dark eyes, with a pockmarked face. To complete his sinister appearance he was dressed in an aged leather motorcycle racing suit. He gestured languidly to a bookcase at the rear of the shop. "Didn't say especially, except they both seemed interested in the first editions. Didn't buy one, though," he added belligerently.

Belinda led the way, past the piles of cheap used paperbacks and well-worn school books, each bearing evidence of some past pupil's ornamentation, to an overladen series of shelves supporting a motley collection of leather bound books in various stages of decay.

"I wonder what they wanted," said Belinda, as she cast an eye over the spines, head on one side as she read the titles.

"I doubt they wanted anything," said Hazel, "just an opportunity for him to chat up Catherine away from prying eyes."

This conjecture was dispelled by the shop owner who suddenly materialised at their side. He leaned close to Belinda, his long greasy hair failing to hide the scar on his cheek. "I remember, he was interested in old books about silver. Collections and that sort of thing. None here of course. Now if he'd been interested in buying old cookbooks, I have enough to sell for me to retire to the south of France."

"Did the woman ask for any special books?" asked Belinda, as she edged away from him.

"Nothing special, but they had their heads together, whispering away. Not that I was interested in what they were saying, but I did hear him mention silver chalices, you know, what they use in church." Sensing he had no sale from either woman he continued, "I can close up shop at any time. I'm my own man these days. Could I buy you two ladies a drink?"

Before Belinda could reply, Hazel said abruptly, "No thank you, Mr...?"

The man turned his eyes to her. "Miller. Mr Miller, but you can call me Max. Visitors to the island are you?

Hazel nodded trying not to inhale.

"Staying at a hotel? Pity. I could offer you accommodation. More private than a hotel, if you know what I mean," said Max, with a crooked smile.

Hazel did know what he meant. "Thank you, we are staying with Lady Sallinger." She hoped the mention of her titled hostess might quench the man's letching. She was to be disappointed.

"Oh? Friends of Melba are you?" Staying up at the Lodge? 'know it well. I pass it every night on my way home. I live on the other side of the island in Richmond. Pretty little spot. Yes, Lady Sallinger set all the local tongues wagging, playing the lady of the manor. Put a few noses out of joint." Recognising rejection when he saw it (an experience he must be familiar with, thought Hazel) Max shambled off to his lair behind the counter, biker boots clunking on the bare wooden floor.

Belinda selected one or two books to inspect. Finally, she gave a gasp of surprise and withdrew a fragile and battered book. The spine had collapsed, but all the pages seemed to be intact.

She opened the frayed leather cover and read the title. "Foxe's Book of Martyrs, including the Guernsey Martyrs."

Chapter Nine

Lady Sallinger paused at the top of the stairs. The house was quiet. Mr and Mrs Lawrence were chatting with Meg and Joe in the kitchen; Marchmain, she had closeted in the study with the task of dealing with changes she demanded to be made to the house; the others were in Saint Peter Port. The discovery of the skeleton had unnerved her and the presence of police and a potential investigation only added to her abhorrence of the whole incident. If word got out, and it surely would, the scandal was something she wished to avoid. Newspapers, television, all kinds of rabble, seeking money-making tittle-tattle. If only they'd done as she wished and covered the remains, it would all be forgotten about, but that girl had to go and contact the police. Melba wondered if she could convince the police to keep the discovery quiet. It was worth a try, but of course, any one of the witnesses to the unearthing had the ability to spread the news. She could ask them to remain quiet, not spread the news, but there was no guarantee they would agree and social media had become such a curse the whole world would know of it. With a glance down the stairs to confirm she was alone, Melba made a slow progression down the corridor and past the bedrooms. The door to the priest's room stood ajar. An impulsive thought came to her mind and with quickened step she pushed the door open and entered.

As Belinda prepared herself for the confrontation with Lady Sallinger she thought back over the question Hazel had raised; why Melba had seemed so keen to rebury the skeleton and hush it up. If it were from Tudor times, surely it would have been of interest to a historical society, unless...unless Melba knew it was of more recent times? And if that was the case, did she know who the baby was? Hers? That seemed unlikely as it was only recently that she had taken possession of the Lodge.

But her husband, Sir Randolph had owned if for some years or at least one of his companies had. Was it possible he had sired an unwanted child? And had it buried here in an out-of-the-way spot? That was possible...and did Melba know about it? Learn of a 'love-child' born to a mistress of Sir Randolph? Given her background, a husband having a mistress was not a scandal and she could have turned a blind eye to the affair...but an offspring might have been another matter. Did they pay the mistress off to get rid of the child? Sir Randolph could have arranged for her to be confined to the island until the child was born and then dispose of it. And who would know? No one...except Ms Massey. Was that also possible? She had been the caretaker of the Lodge for many years, had been retained by the company when they purchased it and stayed on after Sir Randolph bought it. Had she been paid to keep the secret? The more Belinda thought about it, it seemed Ms Massey might know much more than just where the body was buried.

"If you are to marry my son there is one thing you must know. I will not tolerate insubordination. Bringing the police into this house without my permission, I regard as an act of defiance."

Melba was resting on her four-poster bed, the remnants of a light supper on a silver tray nearby. Her physical demeanour suggested a stormy interrogation of her future daughter-in-law.

Belinda, standing at the foot of the bed, stood her ground.

"Lady Sallinger, to not report finding a skeleton would be unacceptable. I know you suggest it was buried long ago, but even that should be reported to the police. What if the skeleton was not old but buried more recently? The police must investigate. Who knows? It may have been a murder."

Melba's reaction to the suggestion it was murder brought the result Belinda was seeking. Clutching her breast and hastily taking a sip of water from a nearby glass, she looked at Belinda with a mixture of shock, suspicion, and disfavour.

"Young lady, you know nothing and have opened a Pandora's Box. If word reaches the press, there will be serious repercussions and I for one will not stand idly by and let it happen."

There was a long, strained silence as the two women looked at each other, both reassessing their original impressions.

Finally Melba replaced the water glass on the bedside table, rearranged the front of her nightgown, and looked Belinda up and down.

"We will say no more about it," she said in a voice Belinda felt was being reined in and taking some strength to contain her artificial calm. "What is done, is done. We will await the results from the police. In the meantime, there is your wedding to consider." The calm began to retreat and her more familiar bombastic manner asserted itself. "I understand you are critical of and upset with, Mark's sudden departure to attend an urgent business matter.

"As his wife I expect you to accept the fact he will fly off without a moment's notice. That is the way when you are responsible for large companies and Mark shouldered that responsibility when he inherited them from his father. There is always some unexpected hindrance that demands a firm hand. My own husband was constantly being summoned to all parts of the world; indeed, sometimes he would be absent for up to six months at a time."

Belinda swallowed a smile as she imagined Sir Randolph took pains to see the separation from his wife was extended for as long as possible.

Melba noting the digested smile replied with a frown of some severity. "So, if you are to marry Mark, you must knuckle under and expect these sudden disruptions. Of course, when the children come along, you will have no time to worry about that, or at least until they are seven or so. If they are boys, you can send them off to boarding school and get them out from under your feet. Girls are another matter," she concluded with a note of disdain in her voice, which Belinda took to mean she was expected to only produce male heirs. She felt the woman was outrageously presumptuous and decided to retaliate. "I don't believe there is going to be a marriage. It's all well and good for you to assume that I would be as pliant as you were with your husband, but that sort of life is not for me."

Melba paused as she was about to take another sip of water. She turned eyes onto Belinda, eyes that encompassed years of total belief in her own superiority and the acquiescence of the lower orders.

"I make no bones about the fact that I don't consider you to be a suitable wife for my son, but it is his wish and I have gone along with it. Reluctantly.

"So my advice to you, young lady, is to consider what the alternative is if you reject Mark. Now I don't wish to hear any more on the subject. We will, together, organise the wedding and you will wait for Mark's return when you will greet him as his future bride."

Belinda's mouth gaped open at this pomposity.

"Now go," continued Melba, "you have upset me tremendously and I need more rest. All this excitement is bad for my heart." She lay back on the pillow and closed her eyes. Belinda waited for a moment and then deciding that little more could be achieved that night, walked to the door.

The door closed shut and the bedroom was quiet, apart from Melba's gentle breathing. Quite suddenly her eyes flicked open, glanced at the closed door, returned to survey the room. Melba ruminated on just how much Belinda suspected.

Chapter Ten

The house was slumberous and dark. Belinda glanced at her watch. 2.00AM. The sleep that had embraced the ménage had avoided her and she had tossed and turned as the events of the evening ran through her brain. That, and combined with the fact that Mark was not sharing her bed but working halfway across the world, well at least across the Atlantic, ensured her mind was over-active and eyes wide open.

After leaving Melba, she had descended the stairs to find Hazel and her mother waiting by the fireplace in the entrance hall. A debriefing occurred and commiserations from both women helped Belinda to express her anger at what had occurred. The other guests were finishing their evening meal, but Belinda did not feel in the mood to face them and with no appetite, she declined her mother's appeal to join them, pleaded exhaustion and retired to her room. Hazel thought it a good idea as she was planning to ambush Manny as he left the table and secure his attention before he moved in on Catherine, so not having Belinda nearby as a distraction suited her fine.

A gust of wind shook the old building and the resulting creaks and formidable groans sent a shiver of fright up Belinda's back. She wished she had a key to lock the bedroom door, but it seemed that most of the rooms lacked that form of security. Silly, of course, to want to lock herself in; if her imagination conjured up ghosts and goolies, locks would be no impediment. She smiled at her foolishness.

After another ten minutes of restless fidgeting, the bedroom grew to be claustrophobic and the need to escape became urgent. Slipping on her night robe, and then fumbling for a bedside book, Belinda felt her way to the door and out into the dark corridor. She would make her way to the Drawing Room, curl up on the sofa and do some reading. That might calm her restless mind. Faint moonlight like an apparition illuminated the stairwell and using her hands on the wall as a guide, she made her way towards it.

As she stepped onto the first step, a flash of light in the entrance hall below made her freeze. A shiver of fear ran through her and her chest tightened as breathing became restricted. The shaft of light flashed again. And again. Curiosity overcame her nervousness and tentatively she moved down the stairs. One slow step at a time.

A rustling sound accompanied the flickering light and a curious tap, tap, tap began intermittently. Reaching the landing, Belinda peered over the railing. The illumination was now a small pool of light close to the wooden panelling surrounding the stone fireplace. Within the circle of light – a hand. The shadowy figure of a man was discernible, outlined against the wispy brightness.

With a rush, Belinda descended the remaining stairs, groping in the dark for the light switch. A faint click and the room was flooded with light.

The man sprung around in surprise. It was Father Ignatius.

For a moment, the two stared at each other, both taken by surprise. The priest was the first to recover. He switched off the small torch he carried and gave a twisted smile.

"Caught in the act, eh?"

Belinda looked at him in bewilderment.

"It must look a bit odd," he continued, "I grant you that."

Certain now that she was in no danger, Belinda's breathing returned to normal and she made her way into the Drawing Room, switched on a reading lamp and settled herself on the sofa. Father Ignatius followed her.

"I expect you need an explanation," he said.

Belinda opened her book to give the impression she just wanted to read. More than anything she did want to know what the man had been doing but was determined to wait and see what his explanation would be.

"Not at all. I'm sure you had your reasons."

The priest moved closer and sat opposite. "Well, I'm fascinated by these old houses and I particularly like the wooden panelling. The folded linen style. So I took the opportunity while everyone was asleep to inspect it in detail."

Belinda glanced up from her book. Her look indicated she thought this an unlikely explanation. Apparently the priest did too, as he leaned over and took Belinda's book from her hand, hoping no doubt to allay any further questioning.

"The Guernsey Martyrs?"

A little surprised, Belinda acknowledged his query. In the darkened bedroom, she had grasped the first book her hand touched.

"Yes. I found a copy in a bookshop."

He glanced up at her with a question in his eyes, but smiled and turned the pages of the book.

"Have you read much of it?"

"No, not really I-"

"You must remember I was telling you about the martyrs. But I think I was interrupted before I finished the story."

Belinda well recalled the interruption; Mark telling her he was to go away.

"I remember," she said, a note of bitterness in her voice.

The priest looked thoughtful. "Let me see...I think I'd told you of the three women who were convicted of stealing. They were burned at the stake."

Belinda gave a shiver of distaste. "That's disgusting."

"True, to our sensibilities. But to 16th-century thinking, it was a suitable punishment. Of course, the real horror was what happened as they burned. They had just -"

"May I help you?"

Ms Massey in her dressing gown stood at the doorway. Belinda and the priest turned in surprise. The priest rose. "Thank you, no. We were just having a discussion."

"I heard voices, so I came to investigate. If you are sure there is nothing I can do, I'll retire." But she waited, her eyes fixed on Father Ignatius.

He gave a slight cough, salaamed, smiled at Belinda, walked by Ms Massey and up the staircase.

Once he was gone, Ms Massey turned and followed.

Left alone, Belinda curled up on the sofa, bemused by what had happened. She opened the book on the martyrs but after two or three pages, her head nodded and the elusive sleep she sought engulfed her.

Chapter Eleven

Ms Massey had the feeling she was being watched. The house full of strangers unnerved her and she was constantly looking over her shoulder. Of course, there was never anyone there and she tried to convince herself it was her nerves and imagination, but in this she failed. Once or twice while serving meals she had caught someone watching her; the priest – why did he question her about her name, Massey? Yes, she knew the story of the woman by that name burned as a criminal, yet proclaimed a martyr. What had that to do with her? It happened over four hundred years ago.

Then there were the two women, Hazel and the younger one, Belinda. They would watch her and exchange glances. The younger one's mother was interfering. She was always coming into the kitchen, talking, asking questions and keeping Mrs Giles from her work. Even offered to cook dinner!

The interior designer; handsome but again, always questioning her; did she have any old sketches of the interior of the house? How long had she worked as caretaker? Were there any foundations older than the 16th century? Did I know anything about the priest?

And what were the priest and Belinda doing in the Drawing Room in the middle of the night? Talking about what? Her?

The other woman, the one who arrived with the priest. She was the worst of all. Catherine Foster, that one. Watching every move. She was supposed to be researching the Nazi invasion of Guernsey, but so far seemed to have done very little, just hanging around the house. Twice now she'd seen her whispering with the priest when they thought no-one could see them. No. Something was up and Ms Massey's heart gave a flutter of panic.

And then there was the skeleton of the baby...

Belinda's mother sat in the kitchen peeling potatoes. She needed to do something with her hands as she reviewed the situation her daughter found herself in. Mark's mother was a gorgon and treating her daughter badly. The row between Belinda and Mark was, she hoped, a passing thing and they would marry. But only if Bel wanted to, and at the moment that didn't seem likely. If needs be, she would have to take

Lady Sallinger to task. There was an air of malcontent within the ancient house, which Mrs Lawrence felt stemmed from either the history of the place, or some current malevolent force that recently manifested itself with the arrival of the group now residing within its walls. Which, she could not determine. Then there was Ms Massey. She'd never felt comfortable with her after finding her in her bedroom, where she was certain the woman was intent on searching through their belongings. Since then she'd kept an eye on the housekeeper.

And then there was the skeleton of the baby...

Marchmain Harvey glanced up from his notebook. The initial bonhomie he'd displayed on arrival had faded. Now, in the solitude of his room, pessimism reigned. Lady Sallinger was a nightmare. Her ideas on the restoration of the house bordered on lunacy and he could do nothing but go along with what she demanded. If she only knew how desperate he was to succeed in pulling off this assignment. He had the history, now all he needed was hard facts. This one success would bring kudos back in London. Self-preservation did not deter him totally from an awareness of unease within the household. Ms Massey spread gloom like a disintegrating Flemish tapestry. Father Ignatius had the odour less of sanctity, but more of deceit; he'd discovered the priest alone with the Foster woman in a situation that confirmed some intimacy. And she, Catherine, was a masterpiece of sullen resentment. As for that woman Hazel, who did all but advertise in the press her desire to bed him. If she only knew. If anyone found out! Her companion Belinda seemed to be the only sane one among them – and the most attractive. With an atmosphere such as they created he would need all his skills to produce what was expected of him.

And then there was the skeleton of the baby...

Lady Sallinger sat in the morning room contemplating recent events. To her mind, it was all the fault of her housekeeper, Ms Massey. After taking possession of the Lodge, she'd been obliged to take the woman along with it. And if there was one thing Melba preferred, it was having her own way in all things; it seemed clear to her that the woman was inferior and no doubt had a past, for which she was paying with some sort of mental anguish, at least that would explain the weeping and moaning emanating from the woman's bedroom at night. It woke her regularly and created an illusion which suggested disembodied spirits roamed the corridors. And if there was one thing Melba would not have it was disembodied spirits roaming the corridors. No, Ms Massey, being more or less an attachment to the house, would have to go, along with all the other waste matter the house had accumulated over the centuries. Melba's lips twitched into a smile. But of course, there was the pleasure of persecuting the woman. Ah, decisions, decisions. That thought brought her to the designer she'd employed, Marchmain Harvey. He seemed reluctant to take her advice on the restoration, indeed sometimes seemed not to be listening to her. Not a satisfactory situation. She must decide if he was malleable. The man presented an agreeable image, but Melba felt this was but a facade masking some personality weakness, and if there was one thing she couldn't stand in a man, it was weakness.

And then there was the skeleton of the baby...

Meg Giles was washing the breakfast dishes. From her place at the sink she could see Belinda's mother peeling potatoes. While she welcomed some help with kitchen duties, she was uncomfortable with a stranger nosing about, peeking in cupboards and watching how she prepared meals, always with suggestions on how the meal could be improved. It was bad enough Lady Sallinger was so demanding, without the added pressure of a critical guest. She had enough of that from Ms Massey as well. She and husband Joe had been warned about her by the locals when they applied for the job as cook and gardener. They should have listened. Some said she was off her head; others that she was a witch. Both she and Joe had seen her wandering the garden in the middle of the night so there might be some truth in the rumours. And she was always appearing next to you, suddenly, silently without warning. Gave you the chills, it did. She'd talk to Joe again about ending it. Enough was enough. The sooner she was got rid of, the better.

And then there was the skeleton of the baby...

Chapter Twelve

"What do you think he was doing tapping the walls in the middle of the night? Don't tell me he was searching for dry rot!" Hazel's cynicism shone through her remark. She and Belinda had driven down to St Peter Port in search of a good cup of coffee, having deemed Meg Giles' concoction to be sedimentary sludge. They sat in a cafe overlooking the Port with innumerable yachts moored in the marina, others bobbing across the choppy water, all guarded over by Castle Cornet with the island of Sark on the horizon where formidable dark clouds were gathering.

"I don't really know," said Belinda, "he said he was interested in the wood panelling, but that was a blatant lie. If he was going to do it, why not do it in daylight?"

Hazel looked thoughtful. "Maybe not a lie," she said after a pause. "I don't mean he was fascinated by the panelling," she continued over Belinda's snort of disbelief. "I mean he might have been looking for something behind the panelling."

"Such as?" Belinda was sceptical.

Hazel gave a shrug. "Well...possibly a hidden safe...a secret door...

or...a priest's hole."

Belinda frowned. "You think there's one there?"

Hazel finished her coffee. "It's possible. Remember Father Ignatius told us the island had been caught up in the Reformation and switched from being Catholic to Protestant and back again to Catholic, before Elizabeth I put an end to it all. Seems the Protestants had changed the Mass, which upset those who favoured the old faith, so Catholic families often had a secret room for a Priest to hide out in, so he could perform what they considered to be the real Mass and give the sacraments to the family and other Catholics."

Belinda was thoughtful. "Yes. That's possible. So, Father being a Catholic, might well like to discover one. And the house is old enough for there to be one, assuming a Catholic family lived there at some time."

Both women were silent for a moment. A sharp cold wind blew up off the water. Belinda shivered and hurriedly finished her coffee. "But why would he search for it at night? Why not just come out and ask Melba if he could find one. Do you think he knows there's a priest's hole? Which holds something he wants?"

But Hazel, gazing at the bobbing yachts, was deep in thought. Aware that Belinda has asked her a question, she snapped out of her daydream. "What? Oh...possibly."

Before Belinda could have a chance to reply, Hazel continued, "That skeleton. I suppose it will take the police some time to get their results on it. The area surrounding the grave has been cordoned off, presumably because they intend to sift through the soil for any clues." She paused again in thought.

"Yes, what of it?" said Belinda.

"That hunk, Marchmain Whatever... remember he took a photo on his phone? A picture of the skeleton."

"You mean Manny? Yes, he did."

Hazel turned from gazing over the marina to look at Belinda. "I really want to see those photos."

Belinda recognised that look in her friend's eye. And if she was any judge, Manny had best gird his loins in preparation for the coming onslaught.

The immature bones of the long dead child lay exposed on the computer screen. Jaw slightly open requesting justice, delicate finger bones seeking sanctuary. In her room, seated before it, Belinda scanned the image carefully. "What was it about the grave that bothered you, Hazel?"

Hazel, along with Manny stood looking over her shoulder. She had waited until she saw he was free from Lady Sallinger's clutches and in siren mode, had sweet-talked him into downloading the photo of the skeleton on his phone to Belinda's lap-top. She was a little disconcerted to realise the sweet-talk hadn't had all the desired effect on him. True he had downloaded the photo, but from Hazel's point of view, this was to be a means to an end. An end that was usually achieved with very little effort on her part; this time however it seemed she would have to work a little harder to achieve her goal. The burr under her saddle, so to speak, was who was at fault here? Manny, or dare she think, herself? With this unwelcome suspicion, she reluctantly turned her attention back to Belinda.

"Eh? Oh, I wondered about the cloth or fabric that's under the bones. I thought it might provide a clue."

All three looked at the screen. "Enlarge it," said Manny. Belinda slowly increased the size of the image.

"There," said Hazel pointing at the screen, "there is something on it."

A small dark smudge was showing through the dirt and grime on the fabric.

"It could be anything," said Manny, "just a bit of earth."

"No," said Belinda looking closer, "I think it's on the fabric."

She increased the size of the image and the dark blob grew bigger until it began to pixelate. They all drew back from the screen. Hazel gave a sigh. "Oh, well. I just thought..."

"Worth a try," said Manny.

Hazel smiled. She had another 'try' in mind. "After all that excitement, I'm dying for a G&T. Will you join me, Manny?"

He looked flustered and gently backed away. "I really should get some work done. Lady Sallinger -"

"Lady Sallinger can go jump," said Hazel, in shrill dominatrix tones. "It's well past the cocktail hour and I think the library will make a cozy den." She took his arm and with some force drew him to the door. He glanced back at

Belinda. "Will you join us?" Belinda gave a secret smile at the note of pleading in his voice.

"Later, I want to look at the photo some more."

Hazel, with a smile of triumph, bore Manny down the stairs to his doom.

The room had grown dark, the wind, whipped into a frenzy, began buffeting the old house. Belinda switched on the bedside lamp. The dark spot on the fabric could be interpreted in many ways; just a fragment of earth. A stain. Something woven into the cloth. Sometimes it looked like a flower, other times it could be a shadow.

Belinda sharpened the image but to no avail. She rotated the image. Nothing. She rotated it again. This time, a discernible, recognisable figure emerged for the pixels. Blinking, to make sure she didn't imagine it, she took a closer look. Yes. It was.

Smiling broadly she closed down the laptop and went downstairs. As she entered the small room designated as the library, Hazel gin in hand, was just sliding onto the sofa next to an uneasy Manny. Belinda's arrival had two effects. One was an expression of relief for Manny; the other was an unwelcoming scowl from Hazel. "I thought you were busy with the photo."

Belinda, amused at her annoyance, gave an innocent smile.

"I was." She placed the laptop on the window ledge

"Well, go back to it," Hazel growled.

"No need to." She paused as the two on the sofa looked at her.

"I came to tell you about Peter Rabbit."

Hazel looked blank. "What do you mean?"

"I mean the cloth buried with the baby is a Beatrix Potter, Peter Rabbit Bunny rug. Which suggests to me the child was buried sometime in recent years or so. Certainly in modern times."

Chapter Thirteen

"Because the storm is going to be a bad one. Joe said so, he heard it on the radio and wants me home, and I don't mean to be caught in it, so I'm leaving now before there's any lightning and it gets any worse." So saying, Meg Giles tied a headscarf under her chin and shrugged on her overcoat.

Ms Massey eyed the pile of dirty dinner dishes. "Really, Mrs Giles, I think you can wait until you've done the washing up."

Meg paused at the door. "Well if you want them washed, do them yourself."

Ms Massey bristled. "Don't take that attitude with me. Remember I can have you dismissed."

"You do that. Then you'll have to wash the dishes, and the floors and windows. And the sooner I see the last of you, it will be a blessed day!" Meg pulled open the door, staggered back as a violent gust of wind accompanied by stinging rain buffeted her and, making as dignified exit as was possible, put her head down and plunged into the darkening evening.

Ms Massey moved to the window where the rain was already running in rivulets down the panes. The exterior was blotted out and all she could see was her own reflection. She gave a slight moan and whispered to her image, "It was like this. That night."

The fire sent up a shower of sparks as the new log crunched onto the burning embers. Mr Lawrence stood erect, brushed his hands free from wooden scraps, turned to face the others (while enjoying the new warmth on the seat of his trousers) and said triumphantly, "There, that should see us set right for a few hours. Nothing like a roaring fire on a stormy night."

The others in the house had assembled after dinner in the Drawing Room and sat scattered around engrossed in their own thoughts or activities. Mrs Lawrence shifted slightly as her husband returned to his seat beside her on a sofa. She had somehow caused to materialise some incomplete crochet fragment, which now occupied her nimble fingers, if not her mind. That assuredly was employed in assessing her fellow guests and the feeling she had they were in a sort of theatrical drama where some great secret would be revealed and cause ferocious emotions to erupt. She rather hoped it would happen soon as the atmosphere within was as threatening in its own way, as the storm building without.

Catherine Foster, retaining her aloofness, sat separated from the others who were grouped around the fire on the two large sofas. She sat alone under a reading lamp taking notes from a book on the Nazi invasion of the island during World War II. From time to time, she would look up and observe the others.

Hazel viewed the assembly with ill-concealed bitterness. The reason for this hostility was seated opposite her where Manny had contrived to seat himself next to Belinda and the two of them had their heads close together as they read the book detailing the history of the Guernsey martyrs. Manny had avoided eye contact with her and his eagerness to establish a closer relationship with Belinda was to Hazel's eye an affront to her own desirability and something of a shock. Certainly a novelty but a novelty she felt unprepared for and gave it no enthusiastic welcome. Of course the fault lay firmly at the feet of Manny; to entertain thoughts of another reason, that being she was losing her touch, was something she had decided to decline and labelled it 'dead on arrival'.

Melba was engaged in earnest conversation with Father Ignatius in her perennial exploration of the Church of Rome. It had been considered by her family as a means of irritation directed at them and her constant allusions to being received into the Church had become fodder for a family joke. Nevertheless, she continued to seek information from many sources and currently it fell to Father Ignatius to feed her curiosity.

"So the imposition of Protestantism was a political move?" said Melba, from the depth of the winged chair close to the fire. Father Ignatius seated on a footstool nearby, nodded. "But not entirely from the King's point of view. Henry still deemed himself to be a Catholic. However, Cromwell certainly used the new religion as a political tool, and in doing so duped the King into embracing it, by not being altogether truthful about the proposed attitude to the sacraments as they had traditionally been celebrated."

A rumble of thunder accompanied by a great gust of wind shook the house, which creaked and groaned in pain. The lights flickered on and off disturbing the group as they glanced nervously at the lamp stands.

Melba rang a small hand bell, the tinkle almost lost in the din created by the developing storm. Ms Massey, whose hearing was evidently attuned to Melba's summons, emerged from the shadows.

"Ms Massey, I suggest you prepare some candles for each of us. The night does not look promising and the electricity supply to this house is erratic to say the least. You will find a number of candlesticks and candles in the dining room sideboard, but I'm sure you know that. And you had better send Mrs Giles home to her cottage before the storm gets any worse."

"Mrs Giles has already left, M'Lady."

Melba gave a sharp nod. "Sensible woman."

Belinda gave a faint cry. "Oh, no!" All eyes turned to her. She looked up and flushed red in embarrassment as she realised she was the centre of attention.

"What on earth's the matter?" said her mother with some concern.

"Sorry. I'm sorry, it's just that I read what happened when the women were burned here in Guernsey."

"The martyrs, you mean." said Hazel.

Belinda turned to her. "Yes. It is just awful."

Father Ignatius rose from the footstool and gave a chuckle. "You've read about the baby?"

Belinda nodded and glanced around at the expectant faces. Only Melba showed no curiosity: Father Ignatius seemed amused.

"Martyrs? Babies? What's this all about?" demanded Belinda's mother.

Belinda held up the book she and Manny had been reading. "It's the history of an event that took place here years ago. Some local women were charged with theft and condemned to be burned at the stake."

Mrs Lawrence frowned and cast an uneasy eye around the group. "I really don't think we want to hear about such things, dear. Not a very nice topic for conversation."

Father Ignatius seemed to enjoy her unease and rested an elbow on the mantelpiece. "Nonsense. We're all mature adults, and it is part of the island's history. What Belinda is about to tell you will shock you more than just three women being burned alive."

Mrs Lawrence convinced more than ever the conversation was heading into the realms of necromancy began to gather her crochet prior to leaving, but before she could rise, Belinda continued. "As the fire was lit and the three women were engulfed in the flames, one of them, who was pregnant suddenly gave birth to a baby."

There was short silence broken only by Mrs Lawrence's shocked response.

"Shit!"

A titter of amusement ran through the group and Belinda grinned as she watched her red-faced mother sink back into the sofa and almost, but not quite, disappear into the upholstery.

"But the really delicious part is still to come," said Father Ignatius taking up the story. "It was Perotine Massey who was heavily pregnant and the child born in the flames was a male. Someone picked the baby out of the flames. It was still alive and brought to the Bailiff, who ordered it to be thrown back into the fire. So four souls perished that day, one an innocent babe."

As he said the words it seemed as if the priest revealed his skill as a pyrotechnist; a blinding flash, the accompanying deafening explosion of a nearby lightning strike, and the room went from over-exposed dazzling white to a blackness of such intensity as to eradicate all vision.

Chapter Fourteen

Slowly and faintly the orange red light from the fire crept over the human shapes as they were revealed in silent stupefaction.

Melba clawed for the bell to summons Ms Massey. "Candles! Candles!" The bell fell to the floor, bounced, tinkled, and was silent.

There were gasps of relief from the group as they recovered from the shock of the lightning strike. Ms Massey arrived with an arm full of candles and candlesticks. A match was struck and slowly, one by one, the small flames flickered into life adding some comfort and soft illumination. Manny rose and went to the window. Shielding his eyes, he leant close to the glass. One or two distant flashes of lightning pierced the dark. "It looks as though some trees have been hit. Hard to tell, but I think there's been some serious damage."

Catherine, unable to read her book in the reduced lighting, moved closer to the others and sat near Hazel. She watched as Ms Massey lit a small candelabra and placed it on the central table. Her eyes followed the woman as she went around lighting further candles.

"Thank you, Ms Massey. I think we could all do with a restorative.

brandy, if you please," said Melba.

There was a chatter of relief as they released nervous tension and congratulated themselves on having survived the strike intact. The brandy was gratefully received, followed by a moment of silence as each allowed the warming spirit to relax and comfort them.

Father Ignatius cleared his throat. "As I was saying before I was so rudely interrupted...what *was* I saying?"

"The baby in the fire," said Hazel.

"Yes of course. The newborn baby thrust into the fire to die with its mother. This, of course, happened under the reign of the Catholic Queen Mary and was an example of the Church punishing those who favoured the new religion."

Melba sat forward. "But Father, surely -"

"Facts are facts, dear lady." The priest cut her off abruptly. "They cannot be denied." He looked down at her with what could only be described as a smirk. Belinda frowned; was he baiting the old lady?

Melba looked at him for a long moment before sinking back into her chair. From under hooded eyes, she watched him for the rest of the evening.

Belinda was suddenly aware of a new tension in the room; apart from her father who seemed to be nodding off, and her mother who had her head immersed in the crochet (probably still berating herself for her social indiscretion) it seemed everyone was observing another.

Melba the priest.

Hazel gazing at Manny.

Catherine watching Ms Massey.

The priest eyeing Catherine.

Ms Massey keeping an eye on them all.

There was another flash of lightning and a roar of rolling thunder.

"It's the thunder that frights but the lightning that smites," murmured Ms Massey, as she topped up Melba's brandy from the decanter.

"What did you say?" Catherine said in a sharp voice.

Ms Massey gave a wan smile. "Oh, it's just an old saying, Irish I think. My mother used to say it when I was a child and a storm was brewing. I used it myself to calm the little ones when I was nursing."

Catherine eyed the woman thoughtfully and said in a low voice, "Yes. I've heard it before...somewhere."

Melba took a healthy swig of brandy and declared dramatically, "Spit fire! Spout rain! Nor rain, wind, thunder, fire are my daughters." As if on cue the wind whistled and moaned, buffeting the building. The candles flickered. Belinda gave a shiver. A long, dark, and turbulent night lay ahead of them.

Chapter Fifteen

The candle had burned very low when Belinda, unable to sleep because of the roar of torrential rain, reached for her watch. Close to three o'clock. Or was it four? Difficult to tell in the faint glow. Another glow attracted her attention; a passing light gleamed momentarily under the bedroom door. It seemed someone was up and about. Rising, she padded across the room, opened the door quietly and peered into the pitch black of the corridor, just in time to get a glimpse of candlelight disappearing down the stairwell. No doubt someone else couldn't sleep because of the storm. As she turned to go back into her room, another faint light appeared at the end of the corridor, coming from the direction of Melba's quarters. The glow suddenly disappeared but not before a wispy flash of distant lightning revealed a faint shape. Belinda could not determine if it was male or female. Then all was black again. She shivered in the cold air and felt her way back to the bed. Pulling the blankets up high to her chin she wondered who it was wandering the house. A faint sound disturbed her.

A cry.

Rising and falling.

A baby crying?

No, surely not.

A night bird? Probably.

The roar of the teeming rain was loudest in the attic bedroom of Ms Massey. Sleep was a distant memory as she lay there, her mind filled with suspicion and uncertainty. Attuned to the house as she was from long experience, the tensions of the evening would only increase and the origins could be traced back to the discovery of the skeleton, the presence of police in the house, and to her mind, the ambiguity surrounding the house guests. If only she could remember...

Suddenly she sat upright, eyes wide with fright. It couldn't be? But yes...faintly, just distinguishable amid the pelting cloudburst...a cry.

The cry of a baby.

Ms Massey gave a shriek of horror and clutched the blanket to her. The cry faded into the watery torrent only to emerge again; the cry of a baby in distress. Slowly she rose from the bed, clutched her robe about her and felt her way to the door. She had no need of a candle to light her path; years of treading the stairs and corridor in the ancient house made her way an automatic response. With her hand caressing the wall, she descended to the main landing. She paused. From the corner of her eye she sensed a presence, but turning quickly she could see nothing.

The cry of the child increased a little in volume and Ms Massey sensed it came from the garden. Down the stairs, across the entrance hall to the great nail-studded plank door. Little effort was required to open it. On releasing the lock the door was flung inward by the violence of the howling wind, needle-sharp rain hit her with full force, and water flooded into the doorway.

She could see nothing except an almost solid wall of water spewing from the dominant clouds. With a gasp, she ventured forward, fighting against the full force of the elements. Her feet sank down into the mud and water flowed around her ankles. In a moment, she was wet through, but she forced herself on, on into the rear garden.

The police tape surrounding the little grave had broken free and was flapping like a demented snake desperate to be away from this place of death.

Ms Massey shaded her eyes from the rain, searching the inky darkness before her.

The face!

She gave a cry.

She remembered...

A loud crunch.

Then – nothing.

The blackness was complete.

Chapter Sixteen

There was nothing they could do. Joe and Meg gathered a few items and stepped out into the storm. They glanced back at the gaping hole where their roof had been. The horrendous roar that had accompanied the wind ripping it free from the cottage was a sound they would never forget. With the roof gone the rain was free to flood the interior, and it was no longer safe to stay. Slowly they picked their way through the mounds of foliage and tree limbs scattered in their path, the mud, glutinous and slimy, held them in its grasp, intent on delaying their escape from the elements. Soaking now, their clothes weighed them down, but they had no alternative but to continue.

Finally, the vague outline of the Lodge emerged from the dark and the sound of the police tape flapping led them closer and closer. They would seek shelter in the kitchen and dry their clothes before a fire. In the morning, they would discuss with Melba what they must do.

A strand of the police tape whipped close to Meg's face and she fell back in fright and stumbled over something on the ground. She managed to save herself but ended up with hands and knees in the mud.

It was then she saw, close to her, the almost unrecognisable face of Ms Massey, staring at her in death.

Meg's scream ensured there was to be no more sleep for anyone in the Lodge that night.

The shocked assembly, still in their night attire, had congregated in the candle-lit kitchen as a near hysterical Meg told of, in elaborate detail, her stumble over the body and an almost clinical description of the corpse's facial disfigurement. The blood being washed away by the constant pelting rain revealed the savage wounds inflicted on Ms Massey.

Melba produced a bottle of brandy and fed Meg copious amounts which eventually stilled her litany of horrors. The other guests were invited to partake of the liquor to calm frayed nerves, an offer Hazel accepted willingly and abundantly.

"We can't move the woman until the police have been informed and viewed the body," said Catherine.

"There won't be much to view with this rain. Any clues are likely to be washed away," said Manny.

"We can't just leave her there in the rain," said Belinda.

"I agree," said Melba, and turned to Joe. "Can we cover her some way and bring her in?"

Joe scratched his chin in thought. "Maybe, maybe. I have a tarpaulin in the cottage. That may be fittin'. But I'll need a hand." He looked around the group.

"I'll go," said Manny.

Melba spoke, her voice husky with emotion. "I think it best you place her in the west part of the house. That section's been declared unsafe due to age and lack of maintenance. The door on the upper level's been bricked up, so the one in the downstairs corridor, next to the kitchen here, is the only entrance. I believe there is a table just inside which would make a suitable bier until...until..." Her voice faltered, and she put her hand to her mouth; tears filled her eyes.

Together Manny and Joe stepped out into the storm and made their way to the cottage.

"I'll make some tea and coffee, and breakfast, that is, if anyone wants it," said the ever practical Mrs Lawrence, as she filled the kettle.

"Thank you," said Melba, "and I think the rest of us should retire to the Drawing Room. The embers of the fire can be stirred and some fresh logs applied. Warmth is a great comfort when one is in shock." So saying she took up a lighted candle and led the others into the gloom towards the Drawing Room.

Father Ignatius, having fed the fire and produced a welcome blaze, joined the others as they sat contemplating the death of Ms Massey.

"It must be a mad man," said Melba, "a lunatic wandering loose. I know the woman was prone to wander in the garden in the middle of the night. Tempting fate. And tonight...tonight..." Her voice trailed off. She was trying to put out of her mind the thought Belinda and Hazel were also thinking. Was the murderer in the house?

"Madman or not," said Belinda, "Someone was wandering in the corridors a few hours ago. Maybe we should hear from them."

"Why not start with you," said Catherine, sharply, "you seem to have been up and about."

Belinda turned, surprised at her belligerent attitude. Catherine was rubbing her cheek and her brow wrinkled as though in pain.

"Yes, I was awake. I thought I heard a baby cry -"

"A baby? "snorted Catherine, in disbelief. "Don't be ridiculous."

"I know it seems ridiculous, but it sounded like a baby crying. Also, I saw a light coming from the corridor. I looked out my door, but I didn't go any further. But I did see some figures moving about."

Melba gave a cough. "I was in the corridor."

They all looked at her. She met their stare with a haughty shake of her head. "I wasn't murdering anyone if that's what you think. I went to my bathroom to get some towels. The rain was coming in through the window pane, and I used them to soak up the water."

Hazel turned to Catherine. "What about you?"

Catherine looked Hazel over from top to toe and back again. "I don't spend my nights prowling. I leave that to those desperate for male companionship." She shook two tablets out of a small cylinder, put then in her mouth and washed them down with brandy.

Hazel's mouth was forming her reply which Belinda knew would be profane so she hurriedly intervened. "We'll take your word for it, Catherine. What about you Father?"

The priest shook his head. "After I'd said my Liturgy of the Hours, I slept the sleep of the just," he said, giving a self-deprecating smile.

Hazel, still seething at Catherine's perceived insult, turned her wrath on the reverend. "How very convenient. You must let me have this 'liturgy'. I could do with a good night's sleep."

This time, the priest's smile was acerbic. "You only have to ask, and you shall receive."

"I think we're all in shock," said Belinda, aiming to stem a further tirade from Hazel. "I'm sure my parents were asleep, and it's possible Manny may have been up and about. I'll ask him when he returns, in case he saw anything. Meanwhile, the fact is, there is a murderer either in the house or outside."

At that, a thunderous knocking on the front door sent a shiver of fear through the assembly.

Melba gave a faint shriek. "It's the lunatic!"

Eyes wide with fright they looked at each other. There came another loud knocking.

Belinda got to her feet, took a candle, and walked to the entrance hall. "Nonsense. It's probably just Manny and Joe wanting help." She opened the door and was flung back by the wind and rain, the candle ripped from her hand, its flame extinguished.

Out of the storm, a gigantic black figure rushed at her and pinned her against the wall. She screamed.

The apparition reached up and removed its head.

Chapter Seventeen

Belinda sank back gasping for breath; with the welcome realisation the figure had only removed a motorcycle helmet. It was Max Miller. He turned away and fighting the elements, forced the door closed.

Distant lightning provided intermittent illumination. Belinda's scream had brought Hazel, Father Ignatius and Catherine. They all gaped at the figure as he wiped a gloved hand over his mud-splattered leather gear.

"Sorry about that," said Max, "that wind's savage. Almost knocked me over." He glanced around at the silent group who stared at him in bewilderment.

From the Drawing Room, Melba appeared in a glow of a candle, which helped shed light on the group. She gave a cry when she saw Max. He in turn gave a nod of acknowledgement. "Lady Sallinger? Sorry about my unorthodox arrival. I had an accident and came off my bike. Trees down all over the place. The roads blocked. 'hoped I could take shelter here until the storm passes."

All eyes turned to Melba. She in turn looked from one to the other. Could she give sanctuary to this man? Was he a murderer? How valid was his claim to have had an accident? He might well have been murdering Ms Massey! Before she could utter a word, Catherine said, "I think we must give him shelter. Don't you think so, Father?"

All eyes turned to the priest. He adopted a pious attitude. "It would be the charitable Christian thing to do."

Hazel stepped forward and took Melba's arm. "I think we can trust him. Belinda and I met him at his bookshop. No doubt he was on his way home. He did say he passes here regularly." She guided Melba into the Drawing Room, and the others followed. Seating the bewildered Melba by the fire and pouring her and large brandy, Hazel turned to Belinda. "Let's see how this plays out," she said under her breath.

Topping up her own glass with brandy, she turned to Max. "So, you had an accident?"

Max sniffed, wiped his nose with the back of his hand and looked longingly at the brandy. "Skidded off in the mud as I swerved to miss a fallen tree. Bike went down a ditch, I went arse over tit."

"When did this happen?"

"About ten, fifteen minutes ago. 'Saw the Lodge and made for it. It's pretty parky out there. No point trying to get home 'til the storm eases."

"So you say. Where were you about an hour or so ago?"

"Knocking back a pint or two with some mates." He glanced around at the others who were all watching him closely. "Say, what is this? Why all the questions?"

"Because there's been a murder, and that means there has to be a murderer," said Belinda.

Before Max had time to react, Mrs Lawrence bustled in, bathed in the radiance of an ornate paraffin lamp. "My husband's keeping Meg company in the kitchen." She looked in surprise at Max. "Now where'd you spring from? Another mouth to feed?" She placed the lamp on a table. "'Found a few old lamps in the scullery. This one's fit for use. Lovely thing, isn't it?" She admired the brass base, the cranberry glass, and crystal prism drops, then turned to go. "Oh, and they're back with the tarpaulin," she said over her shoulder.

Belinda smiled to herself; her mother was amazing. Nothing seemed to faze her, not even murder.

The group moved to the library and from the side windows watched the nearly invisible figures of Manny and Joe as they covered Ms Massey's corpse with the tarpaulin. The garden was a quagmire of mud and water as the torrential rain still fell. With Ms Massey's corpse secure in the covering the two men lifted the body and vanished out of sight as they made their way to the kitchen door.

Max turned from the window to face Belinda. "What's going on? What's this about a murder?"

Belinda glanced at him. "A woman was murdered here a few hours ago. That's her body they're covering."

Max gave a snort of disbelief. "Oh great. Just what I need. I've walked into an Agatha Christie film."

"It's not a joke," said Belinda sharply, "she was murdered out in the garden." She paused and added ominously, "And you were in the garden."

Max blinked in surprise. "Hey, wait a minute. You don't mean..."

But Belinda had turned away to join the others as they made their way back in the dark to the Drawing Room and the comfort of the glow from the lamp.

Chapter Eighteen

Resuming their seats by the fire, they were joined by Manny. His clothing was soaked and wet hair plastered to his skull. "We've done as you suggested, Lady Sallinger. Ms Massey's body is secure now. I had a good look around outside. There's no way we can get out. From what I can see there is a large tree down over the driveway and several more on the main road. A car would never get through, and an attempt to drive off road would end up axle-deep in mud. I'll get out of these wet things and then –"

"Then we'd better call the police," said Hazel sharply. "They'll not be able to get through the storm damage, but the sooner we report to them, the better. If there's a murderer out there, they should be put in the picture."

Manny suddenly became aware of Max. "Who the hell are you?" he demanded, taking in the grim, dark figure.

Hazel handed him a glass of brandy. "This is Max. He crashed his bike and came here to take shelter."

Manny accepted the brandy automatically, never taking his eyes off Max. "And you just let him in? When there's a murderer about?" he said, in disbelief.

Max turned from the fire where he was warming himself. "At the moment, I appear to be the chief suspect, isn't that so?" He glanced across to Belinda, who met his gaze unflinchingly.

"We've given him the benefit of the doubt, Manny," said Hazel, "we know him to be a bookseller down at the Port. As a matter of fact, I believe Father Ignatius and Catherine know him as well."

The priest gave a start and turned to look at Catherine, who was seated away from the group, almost invisible in the limits of the lamplight.

"Well, I...we..." muttered the priest, his voice failing. Hazel smiled to herself and glanced around the group.

"I suggest we stay alert and do as Hazel suggested, ring the police," said Manny

"Good idea," said Belinda, "I'll dress and get my phone."

The others agreed on this plan and went to their bedrooms to dress, with Max despatched to the laundry to remove the mud from his motorcycle suit and boots. Melba made it clear she didn't want him sitting on any chairs or traipsing mud through the house, so she waited until he was led away. She hesitated in the entrance hall as though uncertain which direction to take. Certain now, that the others were out of sight and she was alone, she made her move.

Once in her room, Belinda mulled over the situation. She glanced at her watch; 4.30 AM. So it must have been just before three o'clock when she saw the lights and people moving about. But who? She calculated they had heard Meg's screams about an hour ago, which means Ms Massey must have been up and awake probably at the same time as she saw the lights.

Was it her she'd glimpsed in the stairwell?

On her way to her death?

Belinda gave a shudder and finished dressing. She pulled on some warm suedette trousers topped by a thick, warm, funnel-neck jumper. Her hand sought the mobile phone on the dresser. She frowned; it wasn't there. Nor in any pocket in her coat or anywhere in the room. Taking up the candle, she went downstairs. Perhaps she'd left it in the Drawing Room? But a search revealed nothing. Hazel joined her and hurried to the fire to warm herself.

"I've lost my phone," said Belinda.

"Where did you have it last?" asked Hazel, blowing on her chill fingers.

"I thought by the bed. I haven't used it since we arrived and I've had a good look, but it's gone."

"Don't worry, I'll get mine," said Hazel, as she moved to the staircase and was heard thumping her way to her room.

Belinda had another search but to no avail. She hurried to the library, then to Melba's Morning Room, but there was no sign of her phone. Deep in thought she returned to the Drawing Room as Hazel entered. "It's strange. My phone's vanished as well," said Hazel, her brow furrowed in thought. "I haven't used mine either. It should have been in my bag, but it's not."

They looked at each other. "So someone's taken them," said Belinda, "and that someone is a murderer."

"Well we don't know that," said Hazel, sinking down onto the sofa.

Belinda gave a snort of derision. "Surely you don't believe Melba's theory that it was a mad man who just happened to be passing in the middle of the night, saw Ms Massey wandering in the garden at the height of a storm, and thought, 'Oh goody, just what I'm looking for' and couldn't pass up the opportunity to despatch her?"

Hazel gave her a plaintive look. "Maybe, but I'd prefer it to be the case."

"Good grief, what are you on about?"

"Because if it wasn't a mad man it does mean it was one of us. Someone in the house."

"I can see no fault in your logic," said Belinda archly.

Hazel looked peevish and inspected her fingernails. "Well...it's just...it's just that I would hate to suspect Manny." She looked up to Belinda with soulful eyes.

Belinda gave a short, sharp laugh. "Hazel, you idiot. We have to face the fact he could be the killer, no matter how much you fancy him."

"But he agreed we should contact the police," said Hazel defensively, "would he do that if he was guilty? I refuse to believe he is a murderer."

"He could very well do that to put us off his trail. Make us think he was a concerned citizen, whereas he is the guilty one. But the interesting thing is, if he is the killer, why did he murder Ms Massey?"

"Exactly. That's my point. He's only been here a few days, what could he possibly know about the old woman? In fact, who could know anything about her? Apart from Melba, and she's only been here for what, a few weeks? Until she took over the Lodge, she'd never met the woman."

Belinda shrugged. "So we assume, but we have no real confirmation of that. How do we know she didn't visit with her husband at some time when it was owned by the company he was Chairman of? Massey has been here a long time, remember."

Hazel sniggered. "Are you actually suggesting Lady Sallinger tottered out into the storm and bashed the housekeeper to death? For what reason?"

"She watered the sherry?" said Belinda with a laugh. But she was soon serious again. "I know it's unlikely Melba actually, physically struck and killed Ms Massey, but she could have arranged for someone to do it for her."

Hazel looked thoughtful. "Hmm...yes, it's possible. I suppose Mark would know if his mother had ever stayed at the Lodge previously." She glanced over to Belinda. "Have you heard from him? Mark?"

Belinda shook her head. "No. And I don't want to," she replied sharply. "But getting back to his mother, if she did arrange for someone to commit the murder on her behalf, the question is, why and who?"

"As you say, that's the question. Meanwhile, what about the others?"

Before Belinda could answer, Manny entered from the entrance hall, and suddenly, for Hazel at least, the murder seemed mundane. She edged close to him, which caused him to shy away. He fell back onto the sofa, an unfortunate move, as it allowed Hazel to join him. "I think you were marvellous, going out into the storm like that, to recover the corpse," she purred.

Manny gave her a look of disbelief, struggled to his feet and stood with his back to the fire. "If either of you has a phone, I'll ring the police. I can't find mine."

Belinda, under Hazel's envious gaze, joined him. "No luck there, I'm afraid. Both our phones are missing as well."

Manny frowned. "Right," he said thoughtfully, "let's see if anyone else has a phone. If they've all disappeared, it means -"

"It means someone doesn't want us to contact the police," said Belinda, "and until the storm damage clears, there's no way we can." She knew her parents didn't have a phone, so it remained to see if the Giles', Max, Catherine or the priest had one.

Melba and Father Ignatius met at the top of the stairs. As they descended, Melba said, "Father, I'm deeply distressed with the murder of Ms Massey. To be cut down like that with no preparation, spiritual preparation, I mean. I doubt the woman was a Catholic, but I wonder if you would say a Mass for her, to quieten her soul."

Father Ignatius stopped on the landing. "What? Say Mass? Here? Oh no, I couldn't do that."

Melba turned to him. "But surely you can? You don't need an altar and all the paraphernalia, do you? Just some bread and wine and the liturgy?"

The priest gave a snigger. "Oh, no. If she wasn't a Catholic, well...I'm afraid it's impossible." With a smirk on his face, he tripped lightly down the remaining stairs.

Lady Sallinger clutched at the railing, her face draining of colour. With unsteady steps, she descended into the entrance hall, her eyes narrowing in speculation as she drew a shawl over her shoulders.

Chapter Nineteen

The early morning light, masked by the flooding rain, made little impact in the gloomy rooms. Mrs Lawrence arrived in the Drawing Room, bearing a tray with tea, coffee and hot scones. Father Ignatius followed her in and proceeded to ignore the others by concentrating on spreading butter onto the steaming scones.

"I've checked with Meg and Joe. They had a landline phone in the cottage, but it was cut off as they hadn't paid the bill," said Mrs Lawrence.

"What about Max?" asked Hazel, as she poured a cup of coffee.

"The Biker? He says he had one but must have lost it when he took a tumble. Must be out there somewhere in the mud."

"Father, do you have a phone?" asked Manny.

The priest glanced at him. "No. Why?"

"We need to ring the police about the murder," said Belinda.

Father Ignatius shrugged indifferently and began to eat his scone.

Catherine walked in from the entrance hall and took a seat by the fire.

Hazel looked across at her. "Do you have a phone?"

Catherine gave a faint nod. "I do, but it's missing. I was hoping to ring the La Vallette military museum once the storm cleared, to arrange a visit. When I looked for it just now it had gone. I must have dropped it somewhere."

"It's not as simple as that," said Manny, "we are all missing our phones."

"Wait," said Belinda, "my laptop. We can use that. Now where did I..." She frowned. "The library. I left it last night."

But it was not there.

Hazel and Belinda stood at the library window. "I left it here, remember? You and Manny were talking and I told you about the Bunny Rug in the photo," said Belinda.

"We were all in here just now, watching them remove Ms Massey's corpse. Any one of us could have taken it," said Hazel. "It seems clear we aren't meant to contact the police, which means...I'm not sure what it means."

"Surely it means the murderer is trying to stop us?"

"Well of course, that goes without saying. But why? Why delay the police knowing about the murder?"

"To give them time to escape?"

Hazel shook her head. "No, they could escape at any time, storm or no storm. Whoever it is, seems to be buying time. But why? Are they planning something else? Another murder?"

Belinda gave a shiver. "You don't think that, do you?"

Hazel massaged her forehead. "Who knows. But I suspect it is something else. Something that is incomplete. Something still to be resolved."

"Such as?"

"How the hell do I know?" snapped Hazel. "That's what we have to find out."

There was silence for a moment. "There must be some way we can contact the police," said Belinda despondently. Then she brightened. "Hazel! Why didn't I think of it before?"

"What?"

"Melba has a laptop in her Morning Room. I saw it there."

Melba, sitting in the flickering light of a candle, was deep in thought and barely registered the arrival of Belinda and Hazel.

"Lady Sallinger, may we use your laptop. We must let the police know of the murder," said Hazel.

Melba looked at them with blank, unseeing eyes. "What? Oh...yes..."

Her voice trailed off and she turned away to be lost in thought again.

Belinda snatched up the laptop and opened it. "Oh, no. The battery's flat."

Melba slowly came out of her reverie. "Is it no good?" she said in a weary voice. "I can never get used to these modern contraptions. Mark gave it to me so we could keep in contact. The old phone here is broken and he thought that machine would be better for me. I must have forgotten to turn it off after I sent a message when he was in Paris the other day." She waved a limp hand across her face.

Belinda studied her. The older woman was looking deflated; much of her domineering manner had faded and she sat with shoulders hunched, as though bearing a heavy weight.

"Are you ill?" said Belinda, as she sat beside her.

Melba grasped her hand and held it tightly. "There is evil in this house," she whispered.

Hazel rolled her eyes. Considering there was a corpse laid out in the West Wing, it was a pretty good bet she thought; not to mention a murderer on the loose.

Melba continued, "The priest... Father Ignatius."

"What about him?" said Belinda, giving a glance to Hazel.

Melba moved her head from side to side, her eyes darting around as though searching for an answer. "Something very strange. I asked him to say a Mass for Ms Massey's soul, and he refused."

"Was she a Catholic?" said Hazel.

"Not that I know of..."

"Well, in that case, I suppose he didn't think he could."

Melba shook her head. "No...no. Aside from Ms Massey, he could have said a Mass for me."

"But you're not a Catholic, either," said Belinda.

Melba was silent for a moment and looked Belinda in the eye. "Yes, I am. Oh, the family don't know, they always thought I was playing some sort of game. They didn't realise I was serious."

Belinda took a deep breath. "Right, so could there be another reason he declined to say the Mass?"

"I can think of one," said Hazel, slyly.

"And another thing," said Melba, vigorously. "The baby thrown into the fire."

Belinda and Hazel looked at each other; both had the same thought. Melba was losing the plot. "What about it?" said Belinda.

"Well, he seems to think the story is true."

"Isn't it?"

Melba shook her head. "No. Well, let's say it is open to question. Certainly the women were burned at the stake, but was a baby born? Certain historians think otherwise, and Father Ignatius, as a Catholic priest, should have been aware of it."

"Why? What do you think happened?"

"It all has to do with the old and new religion. At the time the women were convicted and burned, Catholic Queen Mary was on the throne, yet there were many who wished for the return of the new Protestant faith. The murder of a newborn infant we regard as monstrous, and I'm sure it was for the people of Guernsey at the time. Whoever carried out the deed of throwing the baby into the fire would be hated, which is exactly what the local Protestants wanted. To hold Mary and the Catholic Church responsible for the barbarous act."

"So it was a lie. A political move?" said Belinda.

"Exactly, an invention," said Melba, with a confirming nod. "The point is, Father Ignatius must know of this, yet last night he indicated he believed it to be true."

"Maybe he hadn't heard your version of what happened?" said Hazel.

Melba glared at her. "Rubbish. We had a discussion back in London when I told him I was moving here to Guernsey."

"How did you come to meet him," said Belinda.

"After I had converted, he contacted me and we had talks about religion."

"Did you know anything about his background?"

Melba looked sheepish. "Only what he told me. I suppose I was foolish, but he seemed knowledgeable about the Church and was very personable. I enjoyed our talks."

"When did they start?"

"A few months ago."

"Before you decided to move here?"

Melba looked thoughtful. "No. Now I think about it, I had decided to move."

"Did you tell him?"

Melba glanced from one to the other. "I can't recall. I told my London friends, and it was after that he contacted me."

"So it was common knowledge?"

"Oh yes. He seemed interested in the house and the history of Guernsey, including the story of the martyrs. That's why I invited him to stay."

"And how did you meet Catherine?" said Hazel.

Melba put her hand to her forehead. "Don't ask more questions. It's all so confusing. Ms Massey murdered...Father Ignatius." She rose, clutched her breast, and with uneven steps made for the door. "I don't feel at all well. I'm going to my room." Muttering under her breath she left Belinda and Hazel alone.

"Well, what do you make of that?" said Hazel.

Belinda turned to the window and watched the rivulets of rainwater undulate down the pane. "Are we to suspect, as Melba does, that Father Ignatius is not what he seems?"

"A fraud?"

"And if so, why and for what reason?"

Hazel sat in the chair vacated by Melba. "OK, try this. Assuming he's not a priest, he hears on the grapevine Melba is to reside here, cozies up to her using her faith as a common link, tricks her into inviting him here...to do what? Kill Ms Massey?"

Belinda turned back from the window. "Of course, he could do all that even if he is a priest. But why kill Ms Massey?"

Chapter Twenty

Max made his way up the stairs, cautiously feeling his way in the dim light. Biker boots made a stealthy ascent difficult but knowing all the residents were downstairs, now was the perfect time to search the bedrooms. The kitchen had been warmed by the wood stove and the aromas as Mrs Lawrence prepared a midday meal only added to his discomfort. The cook and her husband were both asleep on a makeshift bed in the pantry, snuggled under a duvet while their wet clothes were set to dry by the stove; Mr Lawrence had been set the task of peeling vegetables, so they hardly noticed as Max slid out into the Entrance Hall.

Reaching the top floor, he hesitated, allowing his eyes to get accustomed to the intense darkness. The first room appeared to be that of the priest evidenced by the breviary on the bedside table. A quick search through the cabinet drawers revealed nothing, other than some underwear and a cheap paperback thriller, 'Lady, Don't Fall Backwards'. Max raised his eyebrows and snickered. The padre had a taste for the vulgar. He flicked through the pages. The last page was missing.

The next room revealed nothing unusual other than a partly used jar of Vegemite, which indicated it was the room of the Lawrence's. Max began to speculate what use they put it to in the bedroom, but on reflection decided they were welcome to their connubial and gastronomical secrets.

The room which proved to be that of the Interior Designer, Manny was of interest, mainly because of what was missing. For a high profile designer, there was an absence of any work related items, not even a laptop, just a notebook and some sketches that looked to Max to be far from professional. He chuckled. Marchmain Harvey must be relying on his charm to get the job done.

He stepped back into the corridor and moved to another room. The door was locked. He rattled the handle but to no avail. Mystified as to why the door was locked and speculating on what it might contain, he considered mounting the steps to the attic rooms but instead moved back along the passageway to the other end of the building. His need was beginning to be urgent and his hand twitched as he turned the handle of the door at the far end. Opening it cautiously he peered into the gloomy room.

A faint light from the rain battered windows and a guttering candle gradually revealed a large four poster bed, and on it the sleeping figure of Lady Sallinger. Max wondered if he was destined to satisfy his need, but the prospect didn't look good. However, needs must when the devil drives and he edged slowly and softly towards the bed.

"What are you doing?" A shrill voice startled him and he spun around. In the doorway stood Catherine. Max put his finger to his lips, not wanting to disturb Melba, but she had already stirred and raised her head from the pillow. "Who is that?"

Catherine moved into the room and to the bed. She placed a cup of tea on the bedside table and began to fluff up the pillows for Melba. With this distraction, Max made a hurried exit. Catherine turned to watch him flee.

"It's all right Lady Sallinger. I thought you'd like a cup of tea."

Melba lay back with a sigh. "Thank you, my dear. You are very kind. I'm afraid I'm a poor hostess, but I seem to have no energy."

Catherine moved to the candlestick where the wick had burnt so low it was overwhelmed by a pool of melted wax and about to be extinguished. "You just rest. Some sleep will see you up and about in no time. You really need a new candle."

Melba gave another sigh. "I don't think there are many left, and besides, I will have a sleep. Close the shutters. Watching the rain is depressing. I'll be happier in the dark."

Catherine did as she was bid. "But I think you should have some light." She saw the Paschal candle that Father Ignatius had presented to Melba. "Why don't I light this candle? Being so big it will burn for a long time."

Melba looked thoughtful. "Do you think you should? It is a religious item."

"Then it should provide comfort as well as light," said Catherine firmly, as she stood the candle by the bed. Melba pushed a box of matches towards her and in a moment the wick flickered and grew into a solid flame. A heady perfume began to permeate the air and Melba idly wondered if this was the odour of sanctity. Her eyes brightened. "You're right. It is comforting."

Catherine straightened the blankets and smiled. "Now you just settle down and have a good sleep."

Melba smiled back and closed her eyes. Catherine walked to the door but turned back. "Don't forget to drink your tea." With that, she closed the door firmly behind her and turned the ornate iron key in the lock. Melba, with an expression of contentment, reached for the cup.

Catherine descended the stairs and hurried to the Drawing Room. Max was prowling about in an agitated state, sitting for a moment only to rise again and resume his pacing the room.

"What were you doing in Lady Sallinger's room?" said Catherine, loudly and angrily.

Max glanced at her, surprised by her aggressive manner. Until now she'd seemed a shrinking violet. "Hey, sod off lady!" he responded, matching her volume and anger.

Catherine advanced towards him. "I want an answer. What were you up to?"

Max leaned close to her and shouted, "Bugger off, you daft cow."

The raised voices attracted Belinda and Hazel's attention and they hurried in.

"What's going on?" said Belinda.

Catherine turned to her. "I found him in Lady Sallinger's room."

"Is that right?" asked Belinda.

Max put his hands together and cracked his knuckles. "It's not what you think. I was looking for something."

"Such as? Did you look in other rooms as well?"

Max gave a grimace which registered his guilt.

"I see," said Belinda, "so we give you shelter and you repay us by searching our rooms."

Catherine gave a little laugh. "I was wise to lock my door."

"You still haven't told us what it was you were looking for," said Hazel.

Max glanced at the three women. "A fag. A cigarette."

There was a short silence and Catherine laughed loudly. "Well, why didn't you say so. I can help you there."

The others looked at her. "Don't look so surprised. It's not a crime – yet." She turned to Max. "Come with me. I'll put you out of your misery." With a grateful Max following puppy-like at heel, she led the way upstairs. Hazel sank down onto a sofa. "Poor man. As an ex-smoker, I know how he feels."

Belinda stood by the fireplace. "Do you believe him? Think he was looking for cigarettes?"

Hazel shrugged. "Makes sense to me."

"In Melba's bedroom?"

"All I know is, when I was desperate for a fag, I searched every bedroom in Hell, including Lucifer's."

"Maybe," said Belinda thoughtfully, "but suppose he was looking for something else. After all, what do we know about him? He's a bookseller. Catherine had some sort of contact with him previously when she visited his shop. How do we know they are not in cahoots?"

"In what?"

"Ms Massey's murder. Or...something else." She moved to the sofa and sat next to Hazel. "Max searching the bedrooms, gives me an idea. We should do the same. When my mother serves lunch while they're all at the table, I'll make some excuse and slip away. I want to find out why it is Catherine keeps her door locked."

Chapter Twenty One

Mrs Lawrence had produced a vegetable soup, hot bread rolls, cheese and apples, while Mr Lawrence, after scavenging in the cellar, arrived with bottles of wine; a Bordeaux Sauvignon Blanc and, wonder of wonders, an Australian Shiraz from the Barossa Valley. The luncheon was welcomed by all (except Meg and Joe, who along with Max, decided to remain in the warmth of the kitchen; Max could smoke to his heart's content) and it wasn't long before the soup had been consumed and the cheese board doing the rounds, when Mr Lawrence rose and left to get another bottle of wine. Belinda turned to Hazel and said in a low voice. "Try and keep them down here. I don't want Catherine walking in on me if I'm able to get into her room." She excused herself but as she was about to leave, Mr Lawrence returned.

"Look what I've found. Can anyone tell me what it is?" He dropped a small object on the table. They all crowded to have a close look. It was a little cube, part aluminium, part clear plastic. About two inches square.

Manny picked it up. "Where did you find this?"

Mr Lawrence gestured toward the Entrance Hall. "Down by the side of the stairs, in the corner. I put my foot on the stair to tie my shoelace, and it caught my eye. Otherwise, I wouldn't have seen it."

Manny showed it around the group. "See, it has a small speaker. It's a radio."

There was an excited reaction and Hazel said, "Switch it on."

Manny turned the radio around until he located a small switch and raised a short aerial. There was a burst of static and after a moment's silence, a thin undistinguished voice, interspersed with static, filled the air.

"-unavailable for part of the night. Guernsey Police reported over 60 roads were flooded. Gale force winds combined with a massive tide and there are reports of roads blocked by fallen trees. Heavy rain fell overnight flooding many of the island's major roads, making many impassable. Lightning bolts struck several houses and cut power to many properties. The storm also cut phone lines and electrical appliances. Stormy conditions are expected to persist throughout the day and overnight with more lightning and a 10-metre tide at -"

Manny switched off the radio. "It seems we are to be stuck here for some time to come."

The others groaned in disappointment. Catherine watched as Manny slipped the radio into his pocket.

After the disturbances of the previous night, Mr and Mrs Lawrence retired to their room to catch up on sleep, Max and the Giles' were snug in the kitchen, the others gathered in the Drawing Room, silent and lethargic.

That is, apart from Belinda. She remained alert and watched as one by one, her companions began to doze. Silently she rose and made her way to the Entrance Hall and began to climb the stairs. No sooner had she done so, than Manny glanced around at the others and swiftly and softly, padded out of the room in pursuit of Belinda. Hazel, who had been observing this from behind her long eyelashes, glanced at the priest and Catherine, decided they were asleep, and eased herself off the sofa and tiptoed after Manny. She was not going to let Manny spend any time alone with Belinda.

The gloom of the corridor added to the chill atmosphere and Belinda shivered as she felt her way towards Catherine's room. The handle was cold to her touch but remained firm. Why had Catherine locked her door? What was she hiding she wanted no one to see? Of course, thought Belinda, she could just be nervous after the discovery of Ms Massey's corpse, and the possibility of a murderer in the house.

The sound of creaking coming from the ancient wood of the staircase preceded the arrival of a shadowy figure. Belinda, not wanting to be caught near the locked door, moved swiftly back to her room. She stood just inside and watched, as a pool of light slid along the wall, came to halt on Catherine's locked door, then advanced towards her.

"Belinda, are you there?"

Belinda gave a sigh of relief. It was Manny. "I saw you leave and wanted to make sure you were safe."

Some further creaking from the stairwell and the undeniable articulation of Hazel's cursing filled the air, as she stumbled in the dark. She appeared in the corridor, hobbling along towards them. Manny shone light from his key ring torch on her. "Turn that blasted thing off," yelped Hazel, as she stood and rubbed her ankle. "What are you two doing up here in the dark?"

More creaking - and a shape appeared at the top of the stairs. Manny doused the torch light and grabbing hold of Hazel, which startled her but at the same time thrilled her, he pulled her into Belinda's room and the three blended into the dark surroundings. The shape became substantial and slowly made its way down the hall past Belinda's door, and began to climb the steps to the attic rooms.

"Father Ignatius," whispered Belinda.

"Where's he going?" said Hazel.

"It can only be to Ms Massey's quarters."

"Well I think we should share that experience," said Manny. He moved to follow the priest, Hazel clinging like a limpet (and like that aquatic snail, clinging extremely strongly) to his arm, which somewhat restricted his progress up the stairs. Belinda followed.

A faint light illuminated a room and peering around the door, they saw the priest squatting down, his hands pulling at the floorboards.

"Looking for something?"

Father Ignatius sprang to his feet and shielded his eyes from the bright light. Manny stood at the door, a beam of light from his key ring torch aimed at the priest. For a moment, Father Ignatius looked bewildered but swiftly recovered and gave a self-deprecating smile.

"In a word, yes. You probably wonder what I was doing on my hands and knees up in an attic room, tapping the floorboards. If I told you I was searching for a silver cup, would you think me mad?"

"No madder than any man of the cloth," said Manny.

Father Ignatius gave a tight smile. "A pantheist? Or a freethinker? But putting that to one side, you as a designer would surely appreciate the discovery of an item of beauty and historical importance. Am I right?"

"As a designer I appreciate many things. In this case, what is the importance of the cup?"

"You will recall the story of the three martyrs burned here in 1556.

It began with the theft of a silver cup, which I believe was actually a chalice. Furthermore, I believe the chalice is still in existence and hidden on the island; more to the point, hidden in this house."

"What makes you think that?"

The priest gave a brusque shrug. "Oh, research. Putting one and two together. As a result of that I believe there is a Priest's Hole or hiding place and my guess the chalice is hidden there."

Manny shone his torch around the room. It was a small sitting room with a worn sofa, a small table, a makeshift bookcase, and a lampstand. "What makes you think the Hole is in this Room?"

"I'm not certain it is. There are sure signs to look for which indicate the possibility of a hiding place. For instance, you will often find one near a central staircase or a fireplace. Or in the attic. From there the priest could listen to the search party below, and could use another escape route to another part of the house if they got too close.

"I believe a concealed chapel was in this room and in such a case floorboards can be lifted to reveal a secret storage space, where the chalice and other holy objects used in a Mass could be hidden -"

"Such as a Ciborium or a Paten," said Manny quickly, interrupting the priest's flow.

"Or maybe a Mikveh?" said Hazel, archly.

Father Ignatius looked perplexed for a moment but recovered quickly. "Yes, of course. Items such as those." His sharp eyes sought Manny's expression, but the torch light masked his features. Had he been able to see Manny's face, he might have wondered at his wry smile. "As I said," the priest continued, "they could be hidden if there was a raid by agents of Queen Elizabeth I...Pursuivants I believe they were called. Catholicism was deemed to be illegal so protecting the priest and the chapel was a high priority. If discovered, the priest and the household could face all kinds of horrors, from torture to execution."

"What makes you think this room was a Chapel?" said Manny.

"I suspect the room next door was the priest's room, and the chapel was always close to him."

"Do you know if that room was used recently?"

"I'm informed it was Ms Massey's bedroom."

There was a brief silence. The priest cleared his throat. "Well, I appear to be mistaken. I can see no evidence of a hiding place here. But I will continue my search. The cellar might prove to be more profitable." With his torch lighting his way he brushed past them and made his way downstairs.

Hazel gave a snort. "If he's a priest, I'm the Archbishop of Canterbury."

"If Ms Massey's room is next door, we might find a clue as to why she was murdered," said Belinda.

"Or even who murdered her," agreed Hazel.

It took them only a few steps to what was Ms Massey's bedroom. The low ceiling slanted down over a bed, a chair, a desk, and a cupboard; otherwise the room was bare. A red brick fireplace was built into the corner. The walls yellow with age, were stark, with only a faded print of a Monet painting attempting to cheer the sombre space. The cupboard revealed nothing more than clothing and the desk drawer, little else other than proprietary medicines and cheap cosmetic creams.

Manny swung the torchlight around the room. Something on top of the cupboard caught his eye.

"There's something up there," he said. Pulling the chair across the room, he climbed onto it and reached into the dusty, dark recess. His fingers gripped a large, flat purse. Blowing the dust off it, he stepped down and placed it on the desk. Belinda and Hazel gathered around.

The purse was old, the leather surface cracked and worn; a dull gold clasp in the shape of two intertwined dolphins sealed the opening.

"It looks like Ms Massey hasn't used it for a long time," murmured Belinda, as she ran her hand over the clasp. With a twist of her fingers, the clasp gave way and the purse fell open. She reached in and removed some items. A small notebook with indecipherable figures written in pencil. A faded snapshot of a woman dressed in an evening gown. Written on the back 'Mama at a dance'.

Hazel unfolded a handwritten note. "What do you make of this? 'I'm keeping it as agreed'" she read, "lest it falls into unscrupulous hands' and it's signed by Melba. Keeping what I wonder?" But Belinda's attention was taken up with a collection of old newspaper cuttings. She sifted through them and held them in Manny's torchlight.

"Nurse Jailed," she read aloud. "Nurse Angela Massey was today jailed for five years and de-registered for her part in the sensational society case of infant wrongful death."

"She killed a baby?" said Hazel. "You don't think...?"

"You mean the skeleton? I don't think so. It seems this happened in England."

"Read some more," said Hazel, excitedly.

Belinda shuffled through the cuttings, all of which related to the baby's death. "This one gives more detail. Teenage fashion model Joanne Madison had employed Nurse Massey to attend at her home birth. Things went tragically wrong when the placenta separated from the inner wall of the uterus, and Miss Madison suffered extreme heavy bleeding. In attempting to deliver the baby, the nurse failed to prevent the umbilical cord from wrapping around the infant's neck. Deprived of oxygen the infant suffered death by Hypoxia. The Court was told that Nurse Massey had exaggerated her knowledge and experience with childbirth and accepted the position for monetary gain as Miss Madison was a wealthy woman. Miss Madison, who preferred a home birth, caused a sensation in Court when from the witness box she violently accused Nurse Massey of murder.'"

The article was accompanied by a photo of a woman leaving the court. Tall, with dark hair, a striking beauty, she glared at the camera. "Model Joanne Madison leaves the court after nurse jailed," read Belinda.

"Wow," said Hazel, "not something you'd want on your CV. I wonder -?"

Belinda reached into the purse once more and withdrew an old, crumpled photograph. She smoothed it out and the others gathered to look. It showed a young woman. The photo had been torn in half, but there was a man's arm around the woman's shoulder, the male companion having been eliminated. On the reverse, in faded pencil, was written, 'Me with Prinny.'

"Ms Massey, do you think? Would you believe she was once reasonably attractive?" said Hazel.

"And who was, Prinny?" said Belinda. "I wonder if –"

But before she could continue, sounds of shouting and loud banging echoed up the attic stairs from below. They hurried down to the corridor and at the far end, outside Melba's room, Max was beating on the door and Mrs Lawrence calling at the top of her voice, "Lady Sallinger! Open the door!"

Chapter Twenty Two

Led by Manny, Belinda and Hazel ran along to join them. "What's going on," said Manny. Mrs Lawrence turned to him. "The door's locked and we can't get a response from Melba."

Manny joined Max and turned the door handle. "That won't work, mate," said Max, "the only way we'll get in is to break it down."

Manny drew in his breath. "Right. Let's give it a go." He steadied himself and aimed a kick at the door. It gave a shudder but remained closed. "My turn," said Max. Placing one biker-booted foot firmly on the ground, he raised the other foot and leaning in, gave an almighty kick driving the hard heel of his boot close to the lock. There was a splintering sound and the door fell open. His energy carried him into the dark room with Manny close behind. Belinda, Hazel and Mrs Lawrence crowded in. The air was filled with smoke haze and a sweet, clinging odour. From the faint light provided by the Paschal candle, they saw Melba on the bed as though asleep. Manny switched on his torch and moved to the bed. "Open the shutters and window," he said to Max, "and let's get some fresh air in." He bent over Melba.

"I couldn't sleep, so as she hadn't had lunch I was bringing some soup to her," said Mrs Lawrence, "and thought it strange the door was locked. When I called and she didn't answer I got worried, so got Max to see if he could help."

Manny turned to them. "No one can help now. Melba's dead."

Mrs Lawrence gasped and turned away. Belinda moved to the bed and looked down at the woman who was to have been her mother-in-law.

"Dead? How?" said Belinda. The old lady looked peaceful and Belinda was surprised to see a small smile on her lips although there were tears on her cheeks.

"Probably her heart," said Hazel, "she was always going on about her ticker."

Belinda made a grimace of irritation. She would have to contact Mark, the last thing in the world she wanted, but she must tell him, and she couldn't do that until the storms had passed. The group stood around the bed in a moment of respect. Manny reached over and drew the sheet over Melba's face.

Hazel said, "Why would she lock the door?" She looked at the broken lock, but there was no key there; nor was it on the floor, either inside or outside the room. "The key's missing," she said.

Belinda gave a cough; the nebulous smoke was irritating her throat. "What's that sickly smell?"

"I think it's perfume coming from the candle," said Manny. He blew the candle out. Now only his torch lit the room and cast elongated shadows on the walls. "We can do nothing now until we contact the police; we have two deaths to report, one a murder and one..." He left the comment unfinished. Belinda glanced at him. Did he think Melba had been murdered too? She moved to the table by the bed. A cup, half filled with tea, was resting askew on a saucer.

Belinda gathered the household together in the Drawing Room and informed them of Melba's death. Meg Giles, already distraught from finding Ms Massey's corpse, exhibited an excellent object lesson in hysteria and had to be consoled by her husband, who escorted her back to the kitchen where he knew some brandy would calm his wife – and his thirst. Those remaining muttered doleful trivialities, each searching for some integrity in their eulogy, for as Belinda observed, no one in the house really knew Melba – except, of course, Father Ignatius. She took the priest by the arm.

"Father, may I speak with you a moment." She led him to the Morning Room and closed the door behind them. "I wonder if you would perform the last rights and say a Mass for Lady Sallinger. As a Catholic, I'm sure she would have wanted it."

Father Ignatius drew back a little. "A Catholic? No, she wasn't."

Belinda frowned. "But she was. She told me just this morning."

The priest looked confused. "She told you? But I never knew..."

"But surely, Father, you had all those conversations about the Church with her. She must have told you. You must have known."

Father Ignatius shook his head and walked to the window, his back towards Belinda. "No. We discussed her converting, but as far as I know she never did."

Belinda sensed the priest was concealing something. "I find that odd. You spent a lot of time with her. However, I believe she was telling the truth and I'd be pleased if you would perform the last rites for her."

The priest was silent for a moment and then turned to Belinda. "Very well, if you insist."

"One thing. Melba had not told anyone else of her conversion, so I think we should keep that a secret for the moment."

Father Ignatius gave a slight smile. "Agreed. In that case, I will perform the rites alone. That way the others need not know of it."

Belinda led the priest along the corridor to Melba's room. "The door will not close properly. The lock was damaged when we had to break it down."

They entered the bedroom, chill now as the window remained open and cold air filled the room. They both shivered. The perfume from the Paschal candle was now faint. Belinda closed the window and picked up the candle. "I'll light this so you can see what you're doing."

Father Ignatius stepped forward hurriedly and snatched the candle from her. "No need. I have my torch." He produced it and switched it on. Belinda, a little startled by his quick action, moved toward the door. "Well, I'll leave you to it."

The priest moved to the bedside and crossed himself. Belinda glanced back, then hurriedly walked to the bedside. She picked up the teacup and saucer. Father Ignatius shone his torch on her. "I'll just take this back to the kitchen, and bring you some bread and wine." said Belinda. With the torch light blinding her, she swiftly left the room and pulled the door closed. She stood in the corridor, cup in hand and listened. She could hear Father Ignatius muttering indistinct words. The teacup gave a slight rattle; she steadied it and hurried down the hallway to her own room.

A moment or two after she left, Melba's door opened a fraction and Father Ignatius peered out into the corridor.

Belinda raised the cup and sniffed the contents. It seemed to be ordinary tea, but if Manny was right in his implied suggestion that Melba had been murdered, it was possible the tea had been laced with poison. She would keep it in her room to give to the police when they arrived. Having secured the cup in the bottom drawer of the dresser, she made her way to the kitchen. From the pantry, she selected a bottle of red wine.

Her mother, looking up from a tattered copy of Mrs Beeton's Book of Household

Management, frowned in disapproval. "I hope you're not turning into a dipsomaniac like your aunt Molly. She took to drinking in the afternoon and by tea time was completely ungovernable. The vicar was often subjected to the most lewd display, although oddly enough, it never stopped him visiting. In fact, he began to visit every afternoon."

Belinda gave a wry smile and, taking a bread roll from the table, left her mother to reminisce on Aunt Molly's licentiousness.

Climbing the stairs, she thought back over the recent events. Catherine had berated Max for being in Melba's room, so it was likely she had brought the tea for the old lady. It seemed Catherine had some explaining to do and there was no time like the present.

Belinda halted at the top of the stairs; from Melba's room there came some odd noises as if furniture was being moved. On tiptoe, she made her way towards the door and stood to listen. The sounds increased. With a tenacious scowl colouring her features, she pushed open the door and entered.

Chapter Twenty Three

"He's not a priest." Hazel spat the words out with distaste. "Did you see how confused he was when I suggested a Mikveh was a religious object used in the Catholic Mass? And he agreed it was? If he'd studied theology how could he not know it's a Jewish ritual bath of purification? And Melba thought he was not kosher."

Manny grinned. He and Hazel were in the Morning Room. "As a matter of fact," Manny said, "I've known that for some time. There's something I've been meaning to tell you and Belinda, but -"

Before he could continue the door opened and Belinda burst in. She flung herself down onto a chair and explained how she had asked the priest to give Melba the last rites. "But he didn't. He started searching the room for that bloody chalice. Melba was poisoned! And Father Ignatius is a fake."

"My sentiments exactly," said Hazel, "but if he is fake, why all the pretence? So he wants an old silver chalice? Why didn't he just come out and ask Melba if he could search the house?"

"Because he may be looking for something other than the chalice," said Manny.

"Such as?" asked Belinda.

But before Manny could answer, Hazel butted in. "What's this about Melba being poisoned?"

Belinda sighed. "I'm not sure she was, but there was a cup with tea dregs by her bed and someone brought the tea up to her."

"And why would that person murder Melba?"

"I don't know, but I've hidden the cup in my room for the police to test if we ever get to see them." She glanced out the misty window at the sheet of rain masking any view.

"Well, I think you're barking up the wrong tree there," said Hazel. "The old woman did have a weak heart, and all this excitement probably caused her to pop her clogs. Still, if you're happy to hang onto the dregs in the cup..." Having located the liquor cabinet, she was now pouring a hearty gin and tonic. Belinda and Manny declined to join her. "We know absolutely nothing about Catherine and it seems, neither did Melba. We never actually found out how the two got together, and just why Melba invited her to stay."

"For research on the Nazi occupation," said Manny.

"That's what she says," agreed Belinda, "but so far she hasn't done much research. I still think she poisoned Melba."

"Well, have it your way," said Hazel, "but if so, why?" She took a healthy swig of the gin. "You know, there is something that bothers me about Catherine. I have the sense that I know her from somewhere, but I can't remember where, or when."

Manny looked at Belinda. "Where did we leave Ms Massey's purse?"

"In her room. We ran out when we heard all the noise at Melba's door. Why?" said Belinda.

"I thought it might have some further clues."

Belinda sighed, "I'll get it. She rose, glanced at the gin and tonic, and said, "I've changed my mind. I'd like one of those when I get back, Hazel. That is if you haven't drained the bottle."

Manny tossed his key ring to her. "Use the torch." Belinda caught it deftly and spotted a triumphant look in Hazel's eyes; she realised she once again had Manny to herself.

Catherine turned the key in the door and ushered Max into her room. She lit a candle and offered him a cigarette, which he took and bent to the flame to light it. He blew the calming smoke into the chill air and said, "Are you getting anywhere?"

Catherine leaned against the door and lit a cigarette. "Depends on what you are referring to."

"The chalice, for a start."

"So far, no sign of the hiding place."

"But he'll keep looking?"

"Of course. You know the value of that. We won't leave until we find it."

"What about the others?"

Catherine flicked an ash off her cigarette. "Bit of a nuisance really. Particularly the young one, Belinda. Too nosy for her own good. Keep an eye on her. She could be trouble."

"At least the old lady's out of the way."

Catherine inhaled some smoke and exhaled slowly. "Yes. Her heart gave out," she said, with a wry smile.

"And Ms Massey?"

"The murderer is still at large and it seems there's little we can do until the weather improves and we can get in contact with the police," said Catherine, moving to a bedside table and stubbing out her cigarette. She picked up an old ornate key and handed it to Max. "This is the key to Melba's room. I pocketed it after I took her some tea and locked the door as

I left so she wouldn't be disturbed. The lock is now smashed, but I discovered the key will also open and close my door. Take it, in case you need it. Otherwise, keep up the pretence that we don't know each other."

Max pocketed the key. "And what about the skeleton of the baby? How does that fit in? "

Catherine bent over the candle. "So far, that's a mystery." With her fingers, she extinguished the flame.

Belinda, on her way to the attic and Ms Massey's room, moved along the murky corridor. As she reached her own room, a door further along opened. Instinctively Belinda switched off the torch, quickly skipped into her doorway and out of view.

"Thanks for the fag." A voice vibrated in the silence, a voice she recognised. Max. He had come from Catherine's room, a room that had always been locked. She held her breath as he approached, his clunky biker boots making no pretence to concealment. She wondered if he had seen her in the dark. She soon received an answer. He paused at her door and Belinda was surprised to see he was looking at her intently. He reached in and took hold of her hand.

Belinda gave a gasp of fright. The sudden touch of ice cold metal on the palm of her hand, as he closed her fingers over in a tight grip, was like an electric shock. Then he was gone.

Before Belinda had a chance to recover she heard a door open and shut, footsteps, and Catherine passed close by, feeling her way cautiously towards the staircase. Belinda exhaled and opened her fingers. In her hand was a large, ornate metal key.

Chapter Twenty-Four

Hazel took a sip of her drink, placed the glass on a table, and rested gentle fingers on Manny's hand. "Let me have it," she murmured in a low voice.

Manny withdrew his hand. "You want it?"

"Yes, it amuses me. Besides..."

"Besides, what?"

"I want to know if it's going to continue."

"What?"

"This bloody rain. All this damp is ruining my hair."

Manny gave a grunt and reached into his pocket. He produced the small radio cube Mr Lawrence had found in the Hall, and pushed it across the table top to her. Hazel picked it up and inspected it. "How do you switch it on? I want the weather report."

"Just push the button," said Manny, glancing out the window at the rain.

"Which button? There are two." Hazel turned the small object in her hand.

"Just push one and see what happens."

Hazel gave him a contemptuous look and pressed one of the small buttons. There was some static, a short silence, and then the sound of a baby crying.

A baby in distress.

In the stillness of the Morning Room, the eerie sound created a spine-chilling tension. Hazel and Manny looked at each other.

"Bel said she heard a baby cry. During the night, when Ms Massey was murdered," Hazel said, her voice full of unease.

The pitiful wailing continued as both attempted to absorb this new development.

A loud gasp caused them to turn to the doorway. Catherine stood there, her face pale, her eyes fixed on the small radio. The infant howling continued unabated, increasing in volume and bleakness.

There was a flicker of light as the power was restored and the lights that had been darkened the night before filled the rooms with a welcome glow; a glow that quickly faded into the now familiar gloom.

The old wooden door at the end of the downstairs corridor proved not to be locked but resented any movement, so it took Father Ignatius all his strength to force it open. He did this as quietly as he could; nearby was the kitchen from which he could hear Mrs Lawrence and Meg in a rather tense argument over plans for the evening meal, and thought it best they were unaware he was entering the west end of the building. What noise created by moving the ancient door was masked by a culinary discussion as to the merits of Cottage Pie versus Lancashire Hot Pot, whereby strident epicurean voices produced more heat than the oven.

The priest would have welcomed some heat as the unused wing, long shuttered and dark, was intensely cold and damp. He switched on his torch and the macabre shape of Ms Massey's corpse, stretched out on the table stood before him. He reached out and pulled back part of the tarpaulin. The grotesque features of the woman's mutilated face shocked him, but the shock did not last long; it was replaced by a guttural laugh and his lips formed a sadistic smile.

He shivered, made his way further into the musty room and with the aid of his torch began to check for signs of a Priest's Hole. His lack of success in locating one was starting to irritate him and the presence of the others in the house only added to his frustration. They prevented him from easy access to explore all potential hiding places, and with the knowledge that once the rains stopped, contact with the police would be made, and that would hamper even more his search. The death of the old lady could be considered premature and not entirely necessary, but since it was a fact he would have to accept it and work around it. As for the death of the housekeeper, well that was to be expected.

An inspection of a fireplace, long forgotten and beginning to decay, revealed nothing. The fireplace was often chosen as a location for a hiding place, and as he searched for clues, part of the crumbling stone surround collapsed and he was lucky to avoid a blow to the head from falling masonry.

He stood up and moved to a hallway where a short passage led to a small chamber. The doorway was between two large upright timber beams reaching to the ceiling. He ran his torch over one of the beams and tapped it with his hand. It was solid. He transferred his search to the second beam. It looked solid, but on closer inspection it seemed slightly askew. He placed his fingers on the projecting edge and began to pull at it. There was much resistance but eventually he was rewarded by the sound of ancient metal shrieking in submission. The beam was hinged and as it slowly reacted to the priests grip it send down a shower of crumbling plaster. But Father Ignatius, believing he was close to what he'd been searching for, was not to be beaten.

His excitement building, with one final effort he pushed the beam aside. Before him was a narrow opening. He shone his torch into the black pit. It had been carved out of the stone wall and was no wider than the beam, making entry difficult, but the light revealed a set of wooden steps leading down into a tiny room containing, what appeared to be, a squat table. His breath tight in his chest as he congratulated himself on his success, the priest squeezed into the opening. The walls gripped him on each side, but he managed to reach the steps. He placed his foot on the first step and moved to the second. With a dull rebuke that step collapsed, sending the priest down into the void. His head struck the table. The torch clattered to the stone floor and was extinguished. Clutching his head, he turned back to the steps. Through his pain, he saw a shadowy figure standing at the top. But darkness swamped him, and he passed out.

Chapter Twenty-Five

In the attic room rain running down the chimney into the small fireplace provided a mournful refrain that added much to the existing gloom. Belinda gathered Ms Massey's purse and tucked in the various papers they had inspected previously. She did this automatically as her mind was still questioning Max's action in pressing the key into her hand. He had come from Catherine's room. Was it the key to her door? If so, why did Max want her to have it?

Several newspaper cuttings fell to the floor, and she picked them up. Peering at them in the dim light she saw one was a photo of a crashed car. Its front end had been pushed in by the force of hitting a large tree, and the windscreen was shattered. She glanced around Ms Massey's room. The fact the woman was responsible for the death of a child must have been a terrible thing to live with. Revenge? Was that why she was murdered? It seemed unlikely. Years had passed since the trial, and the young model had some revenge when Ms Massey was jailed for five years. It was all so long ago. Besides, who's to say the Madison dead infant was behind the murder? There were other people in Ms

Massey's life. The photos in the purse proved that.

Prinny?

Who was he?

Had he come back to kill her?

And if so, where was he now?

With these thoughts in her mind, Belinda descended the attic stairs to the corridor below. Moving towards the staircase, she paused outside Catherine's door. The heavy key was still in her hand. She tried the handle, but the door was locked. Without hesitation, Belinda tucked the purse under her arm; a turn of the key and the door opened. With a fervent prayer that Catharine would not return, she made her way into the room. The smell of stale smoke overwhelmed her as she began a search. A search – for what?

Manny switched off the recording of the distressed baby. For a moment, there was silence. Hazel cast a distrustful eye over Catherine. "Do you know anything about this?"

Catherine bridled. "What makes you think I'd know anything?"

"Just checking. We're trying to see how it fits in with the fact a murderer is on the loose; there are two corpses in a matter of two days -"

"Lady Sallinger wasn't murdered," said Catherine, sharply.

Hazel's eyebrows moved northerly. "Oh? Are you in a position to confirm that?"

Catherine hesitated a moment, and for Hazel, she was lost. "Oh...I think you'll find she died from natural causes," said Catherine, defiantly.

Hazel gave a grunt indicating disbelief. "Let's put that to one side for the moment. What connection do you have with Father Ignatius?"

"The priest? None whatsoever."

"You both arrived together," said Hazel, somewhat enjoying her role as Grand Inquisitor.

"What of it? We were both invited and apparently expected to come on the same day. I had spent the previous week in York and travelled down to Portsmouth to catch the ferry. I have no idea where Father Ignatius came from. We just happened to have caught the same ferry. And why all this questioning? Who are you to be so inquisitive?"

"Because we know you met together in the book shop. And it's our guess it was a planned meeting where you hoped not to be seen."

"And you, no doubt, were sneaking about minding other people's business," snapped Catherine. "If we did meet in a bookshop, it was by accident."

"How convenient," said Hazel, "accidently meeting on the ferry and then again while scavenging through second-hand books. Pull the other one, sweetheart, Quasimodo swings from it. We know the priest is a fake, and our guess is you have no interest in the Nazi occupation of Guernsey. Put the two together and it spells intrigue. So what are you both up to? "

Catherine opened her mouth to reply but was interrupted by Max calling from the Drawing Room. "Someone come and help me."

All three hurried to find him lowering the unconscious priest onto a sofa. "What happened?" said Manny.

"He found the hiding place he was searching for. Over in the unused part of the house. The wooden steps gave way and he fell and hit his head."

"Is he OK," said Hazel, as she inspected the man's bleeding forehead.

"I guess so. Just knocked himself out. Might have a bit of a headache later, and I think he has a fractured ankle, judging by the swelling."

Catherine turned to him. "How did you find him? Were you following him?" she said, in a voice that sought compliance, masked by recrimination.

"Out of curiosity, "agreed Max. "I was in the kitchen and the two old birds were going hammer and tongs at each other. I decided I'd had enough and left; as I did, I saw the door that leads to the other part of the house, closing. I was curious to see who was wandering about, so I followed, quietly, of course, and saw him pull back a large wooden beam attached to the wall and then enter a cramped passageway. As I said, a step leading to the priest's hole collapsed under him, and he knocked himself out. I managed to get down to him and drag him up. It was bloody hard work but as you can see, I made it."

Belinda slid open the drawer on the bedside table. It contained few items; some cosmetic containers, a hairbrush, painkillers, and a cylinder of pills. In the faint light, she was able to make out the name on the label, Catherine Foster but the rest was in French and the address of the issuing chemist in Paris. The name of the drug was clear in any language,

Amitriptyline, and the prescription filled only six days ago. Interesting as that was, Belinda continued her search. At the back of her mind, she suspected Catherine of having stolen all the mobile phones. Why she would do this was a matter of conjecture, but she did keep her room locked and so could have hidden them somewhere in the room. But that search was doomed to failure as there was no sign of the phones and Belinda had to admit she was probably wrong. She was about to leave and was closing the wardrobe door when she saw, tucked in the far corner of the floor space, a black tote bag; she had missed it due to the darkened room. Possibly the missing phones? She reached in, pulled the bag to her and opened it. What met her eye was not what she expected.

"And did he find anything? The missing Chalice?" Catherine's eager enquiry startled Hazel. "You surely don't believe that fairy story?" she said scathingly. "If he was looking for anything it wasn't a silver cup." Catherine threw a dismissive glance in Hazel's direction.

"'Doubt if he found anything. It was just a small bare room," said Max.

Catherine turned her attention to the priest. "Is he seriously hurt?"

"Probably concussed," said Max, "what do you think, Manny?"

Manny stepped closer and inspected the man's head. "He'll have a killer headache after this. His breathing seems OK, but it's best to get him up to his room. He should have ice packs, but as the fridge has been out of action, I guess cold water will have to do. Wet towels packed around his head; he shouldn't move, and try to keep the ankle raised. Best to have someone with him, and once he gains consciousness keep him awake."

"I'll stay with him," said Catherine, as Max picked up the unconscious man and headed upstairs. As they left, Hazel turned to Manny. "What now? Do you think he actually fell? Or did Max bump him on the head?"

Manny gave a smile. "I can assure you he didn't."

Hazel frowned. "How can you be sure? You weren't there."

But Manny continued, "I think I need to have a look at this Priest's hiding place." He started towards the Entrance Hall just as Belinda reached the bottom of the stairs.

"What's going on? I saw Max carrying Father Ignatius into his room?"

Hazel explained what had happened, and Belinda gave a nod. "Before you do anything else, I want you to see this. She led the way into the Morning Room, and when the others joined her, she closed the door and placed the black tote bag on a table. "I found this in Catherine's room."

"How did you get in there? She keeps it locked," said Hazel.

"Never mind that at the moment," said Belinda as she opened the bag. From within she drew out three items.

A pair of black jeans.

A black woollen zip top.

A black woollen ski skull cap.

All three items were wringing wet.

Chapter Twenty Six

"OK, so she's the murderer!" said Hazel, "She would've had time after bumping off the old lady, to sneak back to the house and change into dry clothes before we heard Meg screaming her tits off. And then join us as we all met in the kitchen. That's why she kept her room locked; so we wouldn't find her wet clothes."

"It looks like it," said Manny, "but two things. Why murder her, and how did she lure Ms Massey out into the storm?"

"Another thing," said Belinda, placing Ms Massey's purse on the table, and producing the cylinder of pills from her pocket, "this prescription was filled in Paris, the day before she arrived here."

"But she said she was in England, in York," said Hazel.

"York? Well, it's clear she was lying. My bet is she was in Paris; travelled back to London and, along with the priest, caught the ferry."

"Is that important?" asked Manny.

"Maybe not, but why lie about it? Unless whatever she was doing in Paris was dodgy and wanted it kept secret."

Hazel inspected the cylinder. "What's Amitriptyline? What's it used for?"

"It's a painkiller," said Manny, "used to treat chronic pain, such as nerve damage, I think."

"So, what next? Do we confront her?" asked Belinda.

Hazel rose. "Let's go get her."

"Just a moment," said Manny, taking Hazel by the arm and pulling her back into her chair. "Let's not be hasty -"

"Hasty?" said Hazel tartly, brushing Manny's hand away. "What more evidence do you want?"

"It's not evidence I need. Consider this. She and the priest arrived together, and it's clear they know each other. It's also clear they are looking for something; something they believe is in this house. Let's say the chalice was only a cover, an excuse to search the place. So far it seems they haven't found whatever it is they want. And it must be of some value for them to submit to subterfuge and pretense. Not to mention murder."

"Two murders," murmured Belinda, who was convinced Catherine had poisoned Lady Sallinger.

"Well we're sure the priest is a fake, but what about Catherine? She's not an author?" said Hazel.

"I'd guess not. That was her cover," said Manny, toying with the small radio. He pushed a button, and the sound of the crying infant filled the room.

Belinda gave a small cry and snatched up the radio. "That's what I heard. A baby crying. Just before Ms Massey was murdered."

"And Catherine acted surprised when she heard it," said Hazel, "but claims to know nothing about it."

"I think," said Manny, "she was more concerned that we'd heard it."

Belinda considered this. "So if she was aware of the recording, and ...and..."

"And was scared we would connect it with her," said Manny, switching off the radio and taking newspaper cuttings out of Ms Massey's purse.

"What if we did," said Hazel.

"I think I know," said Belinda, giving a triumphant grin. "She used it to lure Ms Massey outside, so she could murder her."

"I don't get it," said Hazel.

Belinda leaned forward, her voice full of excitement. "Remember we heard Ms Massey, moaning and weeping in the middle of the night? And why?" She paused for a moment.

"Well get on with it," snapped Hazel, "why?"

"Because Ms Massey had a secret. A secret that was buried in the garden."

"The skeleton?" said Hazel sceptically.

"Exactly," said Belinda. "Let's say she had a child, and it died. Racked with guilt, she let this play on her mind. And remember the fashion model who Ms Massey was midwife to? Maybe she tracked down the woman who killed her baby and took revenge. She turns up here under an assumed name, calls herself 'Catherine', and taunts her with the recording of a child in distress. Ms Massey, already mentally fragile, thinks it's her dead baby crying for her. Goes out to the grave site and is followed by the model, who murders her."

"Nice theory," said Manny, glancing up from the paper cuttings he had been reading. "The fly in that ointment is, the model may be dead." He pushed the cutting towards Belinda.

"What happened?" asked Hazel, as Belinda began to read aloud. "The modelling career of Joanne Madison, the international fashion model, was cut short today when the car she was driving crashed and hit a tree on the road near her home near Brétigny-sur-Orge. Ms.

Madison suffered severe head, facial and internal injuries. One leg was trapped in the wreckage. It was some time before local farm hands found the wrecked vehicle and notified police and an ambulance. Ms Madison was transported to hospital in Paris, where reports indicate she is in a critical condition. It is estimated four hours had passed before she was discovered, and there had been a loss of blood.

"Doctors have her on life support and are hopeful she will make a recovery, but her modelling career seems to be over. Editor of the fashion magazine ÉLÉGANT, Madame de Tour said today it was a tragedy, as Madison had recently been signed as the face of a perfume manufacturer and had been booked by a major fashion house for its coming Spring collection. Police are investigating the cause of the accident and suspect speed and drugs were involved. Unconfirmed reports claim Madison had died."

So, thought Belinda as she placed the cutting back in the purse. There was another side to the story of Ms Massey and Joanna Madison.

"Facelift!" said Hazel, loudly. "Now I remember." She grasped Belinda's arm. "Remember I said she'd had a facelift? And I said she looked familiar?"

"Where else did you see her?" said Belinda, pulling her arm away from Hazel's painful grasp.

"I didn't see her, but I know Madison didn't die because I remember reading about the facial reconstruction operation she had after the accident. It was big news because she'd been so well known as a model. The operation was successful, but she never went back to modelling. The only evidence she'd been in the accident was a slight limp. After that, she seemed to disappear. But there was something about Catherine that triggered a faint memory."

"So if she is Joanne Madison and came here to kill Ms Massey -"

Hazel interrupted Belinda, "- the old woman would not have recognised her!"

There was a short silence as they absorbed these facts.

"Well, even if that's the case, Catherine, whoever she is and for whatever reason, had a grudge against Ms Massey and killed her," said Belinda, "her wet clothes prove that. No one else, apart from you, Manny, and Joe have been out of the house since the storm broke."

"You're wrong," said Manny, "you've forgotten Max. He was in the garden and the storm the night of the murder."

"True," said Belinda, "but he didn't stuff his wet clothes in the bottom of a wardrobe, in a locked room."

"Getting back to why the priest and Catherine are here, and what it is they are looking for; as we can do little until the rain has stopped and the flooding recedes, I suggest we wait and see what their next move is," said Manny.

"The fake priest is out of action with that broken ankle," said Hazel, "so if anyone is to do more searching, it will be Catherine."

Chapter Twenty Seven

Belinda stood at the window in her room. The rain continued its steady attack on the earth; she wondered just how much more it could take. Through the misty pane, she could see the outline of the fallen trees that, along with the flooding waters, held them captive. She'd never experienced such a torrential and extended downpour. As the afternoon drifted further into a dismal, gloomy night, she lay on her bed, her mind cataloguing all the recent events, including the realisation that Catherine was the ex-model, Joanna Madison.

A moment of irritation produced a frown.

Why was Manny so eager to wait for either her or the priest to make their next move?

And what was that move likely to be?

And why was Manny interested in their activities? He was only a designer after all.

The irritating sound of water trickling down from the roof interrupted her thinking. She glanced at the ceiling. Ms Massey's room was above hers, and she recalled the water flooding down into the old fireplace there. The room must be getting waterlogged. It will leak through into my room, she thought. But the ceiling was dry.

Belinda sat up. Surely with this amount of rainwater flowing through the chimney it would naturally seep down; but there was no sign of it. She rose and, taking the paraffin lamp, stepped into the corridor. All was quiet; Catherine was with the priest, the others seeking comfort from the fire in the Drawing Room or the kitchen.

The lamp provided welcome illumination as she ascended the stairs to the attic rooms. The sound of the deluge on the tiled roof grew louder providing a baleful drumming that obscured all other sounds.

The radiance from the lamp spread around Ms Massey's room, now ice cold, damp, and unwelcoming as a tomb. The walls were damp; the floor dry. Belinda moved to the fireplace and knelt down. She could see water trickling down the back wall and although the bricks at the base of the fireplace were damp, there was no build-up of water.

Which could only mean it was flowing down into another space. As her room was below and dry, where would the water be streaming? She held the lamp closer and examined the blackened bricks at the base of the hearthstone. The base was about three feet square. Several bricks towards the back were free of mortar, and it was through these gaps the water ran. She leaned in to examine it further and the whole base beneath her hands shifted slightly. Startled, she placed her hands on the bricks and pushed. They moved as a whole. Belinda withdrew and sat back on her heels. Was the chimney unstable? Fearing it might collapse on her, she pushed tentatively at the surrounding upright red bricks. They remained solid. So it was only the base that was loose. Reaching in again, she attempted to remove one of the mortar-free bricks. The shock of icy rain water numbed her fingers. The brick move fractionally. Making a greater effort, Belinda moved the brick from side to side. It gradually began to loosen. With unexpected suddenness, it came free, and she was able to remove it.

The light from the lamp was shaded by her body, but she was able to see, in the space created by the missing brick, what appeared to be a wooden plank. Her fingers confirmed this but at her touch a section of the wood crumbled, leaving her fingers projecting into an empty space.

Belinda sat back once more. The bricks were attached to a wooden base; in effect it was a false floor covering...a hiding place? A Priest's

Hole? Father Ignatius had said they were often hidden in false fireplaces, and this one had been covered over with brick, mortared and fixed to planks of wood that concealed the entrance. The surrounding area covered in black paint simulating soot, served to suggest it was a working fireplace and not the access to a hiding place.

The trick now was to remove the false base and see what was beneath.

Gently, Belinda began to manoeuvre the base from side to side; little by little it started to shift as the wood underneath, rotten by age, began to disintegrate. It was hard work, but slowly Belinda made progress. Eventually, some bricks came free, and part of the base collapsed into the hole below. The sound of the debris falling into water stirred Belinda on, and with a final effort to pull the remains free, the whole base collapsed inwards, and she was able to see for the first time the entrance to the hiding place. She edged the lamp as close to the opening as she could and looked down. The space was narrow and shallow. Rainwater covered the floor. A short wooden ladder was the means of access. It would have been an uncomfortable hiding place; the priest would need to be in a squatting position with little opportunity to move. Once inside, the false base would have been placed over him, and he would have to wait in this cramped cavity until safe to emerge; that could have been several days, and Belinda wondered if priests had died here. The thought made her shiver.

The ladder didn't look very secure, and she was reminded of Father Ignatius's fall. On one side wall were two small niches, roughhewn in the stone wall; the top one appeared empty, but the one below contained a dark object. Curiosity got the better of Belinda, and she turned around and on hands and knees, backed down into the hole. First one foot, and then the other tested the wooden steps. They rocked but held firm. A little lower and Belinda could reach past the first empty niche to the second. Hanging on to the ladder with one hand, she stretched down, and her fingers came in contact with a damp cloth. Cautiously she spread her fingers, increased her grip on the object and slowly pulled it from its hiding place. It was hefty and for a moment she feared it would slip from her grasp and fall into the water below. But she hooked her hand beneath it and was able to hold it against her body. The ladder shuddered from the extra weight and with her heart in her mouth Belinda lifted the bulky item up and with all her energy pushed it up into the fireplace and out onto the floor of the room.

Trembling with fear lest the ladder collapse she took a step upwards. The step gave way under her. She dropped back clinging to the ladder. The sudden movement tore it free from its moorings and swayed before collapsing back against the wall. Ancient metal nails plopped down into the water.

With her heart in her mouth, Belinda willed herself to find a secure footing and pulled herself upwards until she could grasp the floor of the room. With one final effort, she dragged herself to safety just as the ladder disintegrated and tumbled down.

Chapter Twenty Eight

Safe at last, Belinda sat on the floor and gasped for breath until she found the strength to stand. With an effort, she lifted the bulky object onto the nearby desk.

Was this the much sought after silver chalice, she wondered.

But she dismissed this idea as the size and weight ruled that out. She fingered the cloth covering the contents. The section exposed to the air had turned a muddy brown, but she could see that the original colour was bright red. Belinda began to tear away the outer layer of the ragged fabric. It exposed more of the original red colour. She pulled back the remaining covering. Before her was a large wooden box, ornate carvings covered the lid. A leather belt had been buckled around it. Tucked in close to it, sewn into leather covering, was a round object about the size of a grapefruit. A third item was a leather bag with a drawstring top. Belinda picked this up. It bulged unevenly, and she heard the sound of clinking metal. Slowly edging the opening apart, sparkling items caught the faint light. She reached in and took hold of ice cold metal. A silver necklace studded with diamonds shimmered into sight. It was followed by more necklaces, strings of pearls, diamond and ruby earrings, and countless gold rings.

Belinda stared in amazement. The beauty of the jewellery overwhelmed her. If the leather bag contained such wealth, what did the box contain?

With an effort, she managed to lift the heavy rectangular container free from the covering cloth. What it revealed caused her heart to skip a beat. Embossed in the red cloth and until now hidden by the box, a swastika. The covering was an old Nazi flag.

For a moment, Belinda couldn't grasp the enormity of what she was seeing, and it was some minutes before the shock wore off. She turned her attention to the wooden box and began to undo the leather belt. Hardened by time the leather was brittle and dry, and Belinda's fingers struggled to set it free from the buckle. At last she released the bounds and anxious now to discover what was concealed within, began to lift the lid.

"I'll take that!"

Belinda spun around in surprise. In the shadows of the doorway stood Catherine.

Shaded as she was, the ugly, pocket-pistol aimed at Belinda was crystal clear.

"I said, I'll take that," repeated Catherine in a husky voice, charged with menace. She moved across the room and as she neared the lamp, its glow fell on her, revealing eyes filled with fury, lips curled in bitterness.

Belinda, her eyes fixed on the pistol as it came nearer, backed away as Catherine approached

"I should thank you for finding it for me," said Catherine archly, "but I'll skip the pleasantries. Just hand it over, or I shoot."

"The others will hear the shot," said Belinda, her throat tight with fear.

"This little gem is practically soundless, and I doubt anyone can hear anything over the sound of the rain." Catherine flicked the gun at the box. "Just let me have it."

Belinda glanced towards the fireplace and the gaping hole. She looked back to Catherine. "Alright," she muttered, "but it's very heavy."

She held the box towards Catherine, whose attention slipped from Belinda in the anticipation of receiving the treasure she had sought. Her eyes fixed on the box; she reached out with her free hand.

As she did, Belinda threw the box at her and at the same time hit out at the hand holding the gun.

Catherine gave a yelp of surprise and loosed her hold on the gun as she grabbed at the box. Belinda's blow forced the gun free from Catherine's clutch, and it flew through the air to disappear down the fireplace. Belinda heard a satisfying 'plop' as it splashed into the water below.

At the same time, Catherine was fumbling for the box which slipped by her and crashed to the floor.

The lid flew open and hundreds and hundreds of gold coins spilled out, spreading a gilded carpet across the bare boards.

Catherine gave a cry of dismay and sank to the floor, gathering together as many coins as she could.

A voice broke the tension. A male voice; full of purpose and authority.

"Joanne Madison, alias Catherine Foster...

The two women looked towards the door.

Max Miller stood there. He held a Police Warrant Card.

Belinda gave a sigh of relief.

Catherine, a sob of despair.

"...I'm arresting you on a charge of the murder of Angela Massey," continued Max, "the suspected murder of Melba, Lady Sallinger, and being in possession of stolen goods looted from European countries during the time of the Third Reich."

Catherine covered her face with her hands.

"You do not have to say anything," said Max as he advanced towards her, "but it may harm your defence if you do not mention when questioned, something which you later rely on in court. Anything you do say may be given in evidence."

Chapter Twenty Nine

"We've been on their tail for the last six months," said Max, "that is after Manny at Europol alerted us to their activities."

Two weeks had passed since the arrest of Father Ignatius and Catherine Foster – or more accurately, Ignatius Yates and Joanne Madison. Belinda's parents had returned to London, Joe and Meg stayed on prior to starting new employment, and Belinda and Hazel remained at the Lodge waiting for Mark's return after attending his mother's funeral in Berkshire. On his arrival from New York, he and Belinda had very little time together and dealing with the funeral and police matters further restricted opportunities to discuss their future. As keen as she was to talk with Mark, Belinda at the moment was more concerned with learning the origins of the treasure she had discovered in the Priest's Hole, and the background to the happenings during those dramatic five days; from her arrival on the island to the arrest of the priest and the model.

She and Hazel with Max and Manny sat in the welcome sunshine, in an outdoor café on the Port. They had got to know each other over the two weeks, due mainly to all the interrogation over the murders and their part in capturing the two criminals, but had little knowledge of who Manny and Max were and how they came to be involved in the crimes.

"Well don't keep us in suspense," said Hazel, "what were their activities?"

Max looked at Manny. "I think you'd better take it from here."

Manny smiled. "Right. It goes back a few years. Part of my job at Europol had to do with the theft of antiques, and Iggy, as he was known, and Joanne or Jo had been on our radar for some time. Once or twice we thought we had them but our evidence wouldn't have stood up in court; we really needed to catch them in possession of the stolen goods. So we've been watching them."

"What's so special about the antiques they steal?" said Belinda.

"Not just ordinary run of the mill antiques," said Manny, "they're part of a world-wide consortium of crooks who steal rare and valuable items for secret collectors. The ones that buy stolen artwork, for example. Monet, Picasso, and the like. They lock the paintings away so only they can view them. They get some sort of thrill knowing no-one else in the world can see or possess them."

"Sounds kinky to me," muttered Hazel.

Manny smiled. "It is, I suppose. But these 'kinks' have enough money to buy these priceless objects, and that's where the likes of Iggy and Jo come in. They steal the items and make a good living from the proceeds of their commission. Money is no object if a collector wants a rare item, so it's worth the risk for the thieves, and they become very skilled in their craft."

"Iggy and Jo. These name changes are confusing. Let's stick with Ignatius and Catherine. How did they come to be searching for treasure at the Lodge?" said Belinda.

"Well, as you know, Guernsey was occupied by the Nazi's during World War II. The Germans looted bank reserves of the countries they invaded, and the gold ended up in Germany. Holocaust victims also had valuables including gold and jewellery taken from them. The gold was melted down, usually into bars marked by the Reichsbank.

"They also held in the Reichsbank, thousands of gold coins from other countries; Italian, Belgian, French, and other European denominations. During the mayhem that reigned in the final days of the war, it's believed most of these coins were stolen, probably by some official in the bank or the army, who wanted security if he was on the run from the Allies. How some of the coins ended up in Guernsey, we don't know, but word had got around that Nazi treasure was here. It was just a matter of finding exactly where."

"So how did you get involved?" said Hazel.

"Our Europol liaison officers advised us that Ignatius and Catherine had been contracted to find the coins, so we set out to capture them."

"But why involve Scotland Yard? Why include Max?" said Belinda.

"As a Europol officer, I can't arrest anyone. That can only be done by the national police."

"That's where I come in," said Max. "Because it involved international crime, Manny approached my seniors at Scotland Yard, and as an Inspector, I was seconded to the Guernsey Police."

"But I don't understand how you came to be in the bookshop," said Belinda, "and Manny posing as an interior designer."

"That goes back to my surveillance of Ignatius and Catherine," said Manny. "We discovered they believed the Nazi gold was hidden here on Guernsey and by a process of elimination, they suspected it was hidden in the Lodge."

"Even so, how did they get to know Melba?" said Hazel.

"Let's not forget they are professional criminals," said Manny. "They discovered Melba had recently inherited the house and was planning to take up residence. Their research on her showed she was interested in the Church of Rome, so Iggy, who was skilled in role playing, became Father Ignatius and, using her religious fervour, set about becoming her friend."

"Yes," said Belinda thoughtfully, "I remember she told us she more or less accepted him at face value."

"She was an easy target," said Max. "And Jo, posing as Catherine, a writer, approached Melba in a professional way, and was encouraged to stay at the Lodge while she did her research on the Nazi occupation. The old lady was way too trusting."

"I can see that," said Hazel, "but why did you become a bookseller?"

"Manny at Europol had his boys feed them false information, suggesting there was a contact on the island that would be useful to them."

"So it was all a setup?" said Belinda.

"Right," said Manny, "Max was posing as a fence, a middleman between thieves and buyers of stolen goods. Although they already had a buyer lined up, they wanted a fence to transport the treasure out of Guernsey. They had been convinced that Max was their man."

"So I became a bookseller and waited for their arrival," said Max.

Belinda turned to Manny. "And what about you?"

Manny gave a self-deprecating laugh. "I wonder you never saw through my act as a designer. Acting is not one of my skills."

"It crossed my mind you seemed a fish out of water," muttered Hazel, "an attractive one, but nonetheless thrashing about."

"More than you know," said Manny with a grin. "Knowing Ignatius and Catherine were to stay with Melba, we heard of the planned alterations to the Lodge, so we created a fantasy designer who, we convinced Melba, was the hottest name around, a designer who had worked for the Royals and some of the biggest names in Europe. Melba, being the snob she was, fell for it, and I was able to join Max. The rest you know, although I don't know how much longer I could have gone on before Melba realised I was a fraud."

"Forgive me asking," said Hazel, wickedly, "with all this name changing going on, I find it hard to believe that an officer from Europol is called 'Marchmain Harvey'."

Manny blushed a little and grinned. "A bit baroque, I agree. But it suited the 'hot' young designer. It is Harvey, but my first name is more prosaic. It's Brandon. Brandy for short."

"I'll drink to that," said Hazel, with a disarming smile. She turned to Max. "And your real name?"

Max gave a laugh. "You'd like it to be Frederyk or Gawayn, wouldn't you? Sorry to disappoint. It's Max Miller."

"Better known as 'Cheeky'," said Manny, "after the old comedian, Max Miller, The Cheeky Chappie."

Max grinned. "Thanks, mate. I'll get you for that."

Hazel viewed Max in a new light. Gone was the long greasy hair and leather gear; replaced by a clean-shaven and smartly dressed, handsome, if rough-hewn, male; that facial scar alone would make an entertaining subject for pillow talk. She had given up any hope of adding Manny to her romantic charm bracelet; it was clear he was smitten with Belinda - and her, him. And a Scotland Yard Inspector as a lover had a certain cachet. She began to engage her come-hither look.

Belinda felt it was becoming a bit too frivolous, and there were other questions that needed answering. "Getting back to Ignatius and Catherine, or more to the point, Joanne Madison. Did she know Ms Massey was working at the Lodge?"

"Initially we thought it was a coincidence she had the same name as the woman who caused Joanne's baby to die," said Max, "but Madison confessed she knew it was the woman. She'd been trying to locate her for years, and it was a fluke she happened to be working at the Lodge. Once Madison realised this, Massey's fate was sealed."

"And she decided to take her revenge," said Hazel. "How did she kill her?"

"Bashed her head and face in with a bloody great iron meat tenderizer," said Max, "the kitchen here has an arsenal of solid old equipment, just ideal for the job."

Belinda flinched. The horror of the night returned to her.

"Where did you find the weapon?" said Hazel, who was made of sterner stuff.

"Quite a distance from the body. She must have hurled it as far as she could. It got covered up in the mud and water and it was only after things dried out a little, we were able to locate it."

"Apart from the gold coins, there was a lot of jewellery hidden with the box. I suppose that was stolen during the war as well. What was the round thing sewn up in leather?"

"Worth stealing alone," said Manny. "A Fabergé Egg."

Hazel gave a gasp of wonder. "Get out of here! Really?"

"Yes, really," said Manny, with a grin. "As you no doubt know, the Russian Czar's family treasures included the famous jewelled clockwork eggs, created by Fabergé. But you may not know some of them went missing after the revolution. It's believed they're held by private collectors, and it seems at least one of them fell into Nazi hands."

"Oh," breathed Hazel, "do you think I could see it?"

"I think that can be arranged," said Max. He was rewarded with a dazzling smile from Hazel. An idle thought flittered through her mind; did he have a wife? But with her usual self-assurance, she killed the thought before it began the growing process of division and produce unfriendly progeny. That could become a matter of serious concern. She would deal with that complication when, and if, necessary.

"OK, said Belinda, "that explains Ignatius and Catherine. "What about Melba? Did Catherine murder her as I thought?"

"The tea dregs you saved proved negative, and the autopsy found she had died from a heart attack. But Catherine had planned to murder the old lady," said Manny.

"How," said Hazel.

"You remember the candle that was burning in her room?"

"Yes," said Belinda. "It had a funny smell."

"Exactly. And that's what would have carried Melba off if she hadn't had the heart attack."

"The smell?"

"Yes. The fumes. The candle had been impregnated with a concentration of sap from the Oleander plant. Fumes from a burning Oleander are hazardous and contain cardiac glycosides, similar to foxglove, but an overdose causes cardiac abnormalities."

"So it could have triggered Melba's heart attack?"

"Inhaled in a closed room yes, but it would have taken much longer to have that effect."

"But even so, Catherine obviously set out to murder her."

"I agree," said Hazel, "but why kill the old lady?"

"From what we can gather, Catherine and Ignatius thought their cover had been blown, and Melba was on to them when Ignatius wouldn't say Mass as she requested," said Max.

"And what about our phones? You found them and my laptop in Melba's room," said Belinda.

"That's a real mystery," said Manny. "They were hidden at the bottom of a chest-of-drawers. Why she would have stolen all the phones when she knew you wanted to call the police about Ms Massey's murder, I can't explain. But by hiding them, she did Max and I a favour by allowing us to keep watch on our quarry without any interference."

Max glanced at his watch. "Time we made a move. The ferry's about to leave." They all stood and walked to the quay.

"You don't mind if I look you up in London," said Hazel to Max.

"I'd be disappointed if you didn't," Max replied with a grin, "but we'll meet again during all the legal proceedings against our 'friends' and a murder trial can go on for some time, time for us to get better acquainted."

"In that case," said Hazel, "let's hope for a re-trial." She smiled and gave him a gentle push to send him on his way.

Manny turned to Belinda. "Are you staying on here for much longer?"

Belinda nodded. "Until I hear from Mark and what his plans are."

"And they are?"

"I don't know. Our wedding is on hold and..." Her voice trailed off. Should she say 'the wedding is off' she wondered.

Manny smiled. "Well, either way, you'll be hearing from the solicitors about the trials, so we'll meet up again in London."

"I'll have to get used to calling you, Brandon," said Belinda.

"I prefer Brandy," said Manny as he took her hand in his.

Belinda laughed and for a moment they held each other in their gaze.

Somewhat reluctantly he released her hand and boarded the ferry. Both women watched in silence as the sleek vessel slid free from its moorings and began the ocean journey.

Chapter Thirty

The car journey back to the Lodge was conducted in silence as the two women thought back over the recent events, and both also considered a scenario for the future. Hazel wearily pushed open the heavy wooden plank door, and they entered the Drawing Room, to be greeted by clattering and thumps emanating from the Morning Room. Belinda answered Hazel's silent question. "It's Meg. I told her to go ahead with Melba's wishes to take all the junk that was stored in the cabinet, down to the Charity Shop."

Hazel dropped the car keys on a table and poured a gin and tonic. She waved the bottle questioningly to Belinda, who shook her head as she switched on her laptop. She sank down onto a chair and flicked through her email. There was one from Mark.

from: Mark Sallinger
<marksalco@cxor822.com>
to: Belinda Lawrence <bellaw@aqz1mail.com>
date: Tues, March 4, at 10:15 AM
subject: Update

Bel,

Mother's funeral went as well as can be expected. Sister Pat and family attended. Pat stays on to sort out things at the family home. Sorry we had so little time to talk. The thing is I must return to NY at once to continue dealing with the company fraud. I'll arrange for you to fly and join me there, but I must warn you, I'll have little time as I'm up to my neck with lawyers etc., However, if you wish to come just let me know and...

Belinda stopped reading and clicked off the computer. She stared ahead in silence for a long time.

Hazel, slowly aware of the quiet, turned to her. "What's the matter?"

Belinda gave a wry smile. "I'll have that gin now."

Hazel poured the drink. Belinda took it and sat beside her friend.

"Bad news?" asked Hazel.

"Actually, I'd say it's good news." She looked down at the diamond ring on her finger and gently eased it off, held it to the light to catch the glittering brilliance, then with a swift move dropped it into her gin.

Hazel looked at her over the rim of her glass suspecting incipient lunacy had descended on her friend. She waited for an explanation.

Belinda watched the tonic water bubbles caress the diamond. "Cleopatra is said to have dissolved pearls in wine. It would be nice to think this diamond would dissolve, along with its obligation."

"You mean, Mark has - "

"No, not Mark. Me. I've called it off. There will be no wedding. And, in the tradition of all soap opera divas, I'd rather not talk about it now."

Hazel gave a tight smile and raised her glass in a toast.

The tension was broken by loud clanking as Meg, carrying several large bags, entered from the Morning Room. "I've cleaned out the cabinet as you asked Miss and a bigger load of rubbish I've yet to see. Although there was one vase, I liked. Do you think I could keep it? As a souvenir, like."

Belinda smiled. "Of course. Keep anything you want."

Meg gave a nod of acknowledgement and was about to haul the bags away when she turned and rummaged through one bag.

"I almost forgot. I found this parcel pushed right back and hidden behind all the rubbish.

Not sure what it is, but thought you'd better have it. It might be something important."

The 'something important' was a brown paper parcel tied with string. Belinda took it.

"I'll be off then," said Meg. "Joe's got a loan of a car and Mrs Grant at the charity shop is staying open late, waiting for this rubbish." Accompanied by clinking and clunking, she hauled the bags out to the car.

Hazel and Belinda looked at the parcel. "Well, open it," said Hazel irritably. Belinda picked at the tightly drawn string and with some effort, undid the knot. She pulled aside the paper to reveal a book. A diary dated thirty-five years in the past. She opened the cover to the front page.

"Angela Massey," she read aloud.

"Her diary?" said Hazel. "What's it doing hidden away?"

"Who knows," said Belinda, "maybe it was something special." She turned a few pages. "Doesn't seem to say much, just day to day things about running the house."

"From the date, it must have been before Sir Randolph's company bought the Lodge. I wonder who owned it then?"

"It might say," said Belinda as she began to read, "Monday. Spent the day cleaning after the house party at the weekend. Lord Woodgate was the last to leave as usual. The Master and Madam back again next weekend."

She flipped through a few pages. "Seems pretty much the same. Just entries of house parties and some bigwig names." She read on in silence. "Wait on. Here's something of interest. 'Excitement, this week as it's known a Prince, will be staying for the weekend. Royalty comes to the Lodge!'"

"Prince who? "said Hazel.

"Doesn't say," said Belinda as she flicked through more pages. "He's back again the next month. 'The Prince was very complimentary to me last night. I hope Prinny visits more often.'"

"Prinny?" said Hazel with a shriek. "Not George the Fourth?"

Belinda sniggered. "Ms Massey wasn't that old. Let me see, judging from the year this diary is dated she would have been in her mid-thirties, I guess. Still, I wonder who 'Prinny' was?"

"Read on, she may give his name."

Belinda flicked through some more entries. "Here, he's mentioned again. A few months after the last reference. 'I so hoped Prinny was coming this weekend. Not sure what to do.'"

"What to do?" said Hazel.

"There's more," said Belinda. "'No answer to my letters and the family have gone away for the season, so no hope of him visiting soon. Am getting desperate.'"

Hazel's eyebrows shot up. "Hello, it sounds to me as though Prinny has been doing a bit of rogering at weekends."

"You mean him and Ms Massey…?"

"A bit of 'how's your father' downstairs. And Ms Massey left holding the baby. Read on, there might be more."

Belinda turned page after page. "Here. This is it. 'My waters have broken and the birth is near. Thankfully the family have not visited for some months and no one knows my situation. Hopefully the birth will go well. But I must let Prinny know.' And then a few days later. 'Terrible storm last night. Was in labour for about four hours. Baby born dead. Will bury him in the garden tomorrow. No one will know. Expect not to hear from Prinny again.'"

The two women looked at each other.

"Well that explains the skeleton," said Hazel.

"Yes, but why was this diary hidden away."

"I've just thought of something. Remember when we searched Ms Massey's room and found the old purse? There was a note from Melba saying something like, 'I'll keep this for safety in case someone sees it."

"So she knew about the baby, knew the skeleton was it, didn't want anyone to know about Ms Massey's past because –"

"Because of scandal," said Hazel, "she was such a snob."

Belinda's face lit up. "And that's why she hid our phones. She was scared the press would get to know of the story and it would reflect on her."

"But I also think she was a little more devious. I bet she used the diary as a means of having a hold over Ms Massey. Keep her in her place and continue to work at the Lodge as housekeeper. If the woman ever wanted to leave, Melba only had to remind her she had the diary and would let the world know unless the woman came to heel."

"A false threat," said Belinda, "because we know Melba was terrified of anyone thinking she was associated with a society scandal involving royalty."

"Phew," said Hazel. "I think that calls for another gin."

"I'll join you," said Belinda as she closed the diary.

"In which case," said Hazel, "I'd take that diamond out of the gin. Don't want to tempt fate."

They sat sipping their drinks in silence. Hazel turned to her friend. "I know you don't want to talk about it, but did you mean it when you said the wedding was off?"

Belinda lowered her glass. "Definitely. Finito. Mark is part of my past. A new page, a new book, so to speak."

Hazel smiled thoughtfully at her friend. Time will tell, she thought, time will tell.

Meg Giles closed the door behind her at the Charity shop, leaving Mrs. Grant to peruse the assembled dross recently deposited on her counter. She imagined, after much inspection, she might be able to salvage a few items of value; the rest she would send to the tip.

A quite beautiful cake tray.

A rather old pewter plate.

Some EPNS forks and spoons.

A heavily tarnished item, almost black, a bit knocked about, but to her trained eye, Mrs Grant was certain it was a solid silver cup.

THE END.